# The
# Buffalo Nickel
# Blues Band

# Also by Judie Angell

*Dear Lola*
*or How to Build Your Own Family*

*A Word from Our Sponsor*
*or My Friend Alfred*

*In Summertime It's Tuffy*

*Tina Gogo*

*What's Best for You*

*Ronnie and Rosey*

*Secret Selves*

# The Buffalo Nickel Blues Band

## BY JUDIE ANGELL

*Bradbury Press*     *Scarsdale, N.Y.*

I wish to express my appreciation for technical
help and advice from George Vogliano, M.D., and
from Woodstock Numismatics.—J.A.

Library of Congress Cataloging in Publication Data
Angell, Judie. The Buffalo Nickel Blues Band.
Summary: Eddie Levy relates how he and his four friends who are
involved in a blues band change as their music does.
  [1. Rhythm and blues music—Fiction.
2. Musicians—Fiction]  I. Title.
PZ7.A5824Bu      [Fic]       81-18075
ISBN 0-87888-195-6          AACR2

A dedication with thanks
to these fine musicians who were so helpful:

*Joe Knowlton*
*Stash Rossi*
*Billy Woerter*
*Tim LuBell*
*Kerri LuBell*
*Eugene Kim*
*and of course, Phil*

Even last July we were a good-sounding group. We'd already been practicing for a year, since the middle of sixth grade: Ivy Sunday on drums, Georgie Redding on guitar and me, Eddie Levy, on the keyboard. The Centerin City Blues Trio, that was us—and if I say so myself, we were terrific. The only problem was, nobody knew it.

My mother changed all that, once *she* knew . . .

She got this inspiration while sitting in our tiny backyard knitting a six-foot green-and-white scarf for my cousin Morton who goes to Dartmouth. She clacked her knitting needles together, put everything down in her lap, turned to my perspiring father and said, "Norman, what do you say we have a party?" She looked at me and winked, so I guessed why she said it and what she was doing it for.

My father said, "A what?" and went back to his paper. My mother talks a lot but my father hardly talks at all. So when he does talk, you really want to listen because even though it's low key, it's probably going to be important, like "Excuse me, miss, but isn't the left wing of this plane on fire?"

1

"Norman, I said 'a party.' A party, Norman, what do you say?"

"I say . . . that knitting a wool scarf on a hundred-degree-day in July is making you a little funny."

"No, Norman, come on, a small party, nothing fancy, come on . . ."

"A party! What for? To celebrate the humidity? Next spring we'll have a party. Eddie's bar mitzvah, that'll be a party. Meanwhile, a party for what?" That was one of my father's longest speeches. He went back to his paper, exhausted.

"A party for *nothing*, Norman!" my mother persisted. My mother persists a lot.

"There is no party for nothing," my father said. "Parties cost money. When there's something to celebrate then I'll have a party."

My mother looked over at me and I looked at her.

"How about a party to celebrate Eddie's trio?" my mother said softly.

My father looked up from his paper. "You want to celebrate Eddie's trio?" he asked. "Eddie's trio I'm already celebrating. He's supposed to celebrate his own trio by mowing lawns and paying me back for his portable piano."

"It's an electric key—" I began, but my mother said "Sh!"

My father sighed.

"He'll get jobs playing after people hear how

good he is," my mother said. "So we'll let people hear. We could have Rosalie and Mike and the cousins from Riverdale and Arlene and Hal and the Cranmers and Harrises from the neighborhood."

"And Liza Minelli and Truman Capote and Leonard Bernstein," my father said, mopping his face with a handkerchief.

"And Georgie and Ivy's folks," I put in and my mother said "Sh!"

"Some little hors d'oeuvres, some canapes," my mother went on.

"We could grill a few hamburgers," I suggested and my mother said "Sh!"

"In the back, right here, Norman, nothing fancy, simple, a few friends, a few relatives . . . *Carrot sticks, Norman!*"

"Don't yell."

"I'm sorry."

"How about inviting Mr. Broigen?" I asked, half kidding.

"*Doctor* Broigen," my mother corrected. Dr. Broigen is our next door neighbor. He's not a real doctor, he's some kind of plant professor or something, but he always makes you call him "doctor" which bugs me so I always call him "mister."

"We could invite him," my mother said.

"Hah!" my father barked. "He wouldn't come. He only goes out for lectures on diseases of the roots of crabgrass."

3

My mother beamed. "Ah, Norman, then it's okay? We'll have the party!"

❀

We had the party two weeks later. It was a barbecue, like I had originally suggested, but it wasn't all that simple.

My Aunt Rosalie and Uncle Mike came in from Riverdale early so Aunt Rosalie could help with the food. Aunt Rosalie is my mother's sister. She and my mother love preparing food, love eating food and love to argue, mostly about food. So they're the ones the family always picks to "do" the parties and get-togethers we have. And long before any of the people come, you can hear my mother and Aunt Rosalie in the kitchen hollering at each other. It's a very nice, secure sound; no party would be the same without it and it always makes me smile, although from *outside* the door.

For instance, the morning of this party I came downstairs in time to hear the argument over the hors d'oeuvres. They got through the puff pastry with shrimp in it, the rolled-up dough things with gooky spinach inside, and the artichoke pieces that you dip in something yellow, with the usual growls about how *much* mayonnaise, how to get the pastry *thinner,* and not so much *cream!* But when they got to the huge mounds of chopped liver—my mother's specialty—that's when they got into it!

"Rosalie, what are you making with the chopped liver?"

4

"What does it look like I'm making with the chopped liver?"

"It looks like a guitar. It looks like you're molding it into a guitar."

"Good. It is a guitar."

"Eddie doesn't play guitar. He's a piano player."

"So? He's a musician, isn't he? Guitars make music."

"With the chopped liver, you can mold a piano. *Then* it will be for Eddie."

"My nephew Eddie will love this chopped liver guitar."

"He would love a chopped liver *piano* better!"

I was standing outside the kitchen door smiling as my father passed.

"They're having a good time, Pop," I said to him.

He nodded. "People will eat up that chopped liver before they even know it's a guitar *or* a piano," he said with a sigh. "And Rosalie will spend hours on it."

"I know," I said, still smiling.

And then from the kitchen: "What is *that* you're using for the strings?"

"Cole slaw."

"I can see it's cole slaw! Rosalie, you better learn to make a piano in time for Eddie's bar mitzvah!"

I left then and went outside. Luckily, the weather was fine. If it had rained, we never would have fit all the food and people into our small living room.

"Hey, Eddie! Where do you want the drums?"

I turned to see Ivy Sunday and her dad, struggling to get all her stuff around the rhododendrons and I ran over to help.

"Oh," I said, trying to think, "uh, how about over there?"

"No, not in the sun, Eddie," Ivy said, shaking her head. "It'll be too hot. How about over there, under your neighbor's tree, near the fence?"

"Fine!" I shrugged. "Sure. Let's set up. Where's your mom?"

"She went in the front way with Raymond." Raymond is Ivy's older brother.

"You excited, Eddie?" Mr. Sunday asked. "Your first audience!"

"Yeah . . . I guess . . . Well, sure! Aren't you, Ivy?"

She grinned. "When I hear how we sound, then I'll be excited."

"Are you kidding, we're going to be sensational!" I said.

"Sure you are!" It was Mr. Redding, Georgie's father, coming around back with Mrs. Redding, Georgie's amp, Georgie's guitar, and Georgie.

"Hi, man, I'm nervous, you nervous?" he said in one breath.

"Nah. Yes," I said.

"A little," Ivy said.

"You don't have to be nervous," Mrs. Redding said. "You've certainly done enough practicing."

"Aw, Ma, it hasn't been that bad," Georgie said.

"The tiles are starting to drop off the kitchen

walls," Mrs. Redding grumbled. We'd been practicing in Georgie's basement, underneath the kitchen.

Georgie's father said, "Now, Geraldine," and Mrs. Redding said, "Well, you're not home when they practice." Then she looked a little sheepishly at us, as if she didn't want to spoil our day. "I'm sorry, kids. It's not that you're not fine musicians, but the noise—the *music*—is a little too much for our small house."

"We'll try to keep it down, Mrs. Redding," I said, wondering how we could manage that.

She patted my hand. "Okay, Eddie. Have fun today. Listen, where's your mother, in the house? I think I'll go in and see if there's anything I can do to help."

When she left, Mr. Redding, Mr. Sunday and us kids set up our stuff under the tree. I had taken my keyboard and amp out earlier and left it at the side of the house till we picked a spot and as I went to get them, a lot of people began to arrive.

Mom and Aunt Rosalie's childhood friend Arlene and her husband Harold ran up and hugged me, and right behind them were my cousin Audrey—Aunt Rosalie's married daughter—and her husband, Arthur. They named their kids Alice and Andrew and their dog Ashley, if you can believe that! Alice and Andrew were there, rushing past people to get to the backyard and the food. At least they left Ashley home.

"Hi, Eddie!" Audrey cried. "Hear you're going to be a big star! Kids! Alice, Andrew! Be careful! Don't knock the table over!"

Alice and Andrew were about three and four and they were wild. I hoped they wouldn't wreck our concert. Georgie'd left *his* little twin brothers home and my nine-year-old sister Yvonne was at Performing Arts Camp. Not that she's that little, but she'd probably have wanted to dance for everybody . . .

"Eddie! Here, let me help you—" Ivy took my amp handle. "How many more people are coming?" she asked breathlessly.

"Uh, well, there're the neighbors—the Cranmers, the Jablonskis and the Harrises." We'd asked Mr. Broigen but he'd said he was busy. He was always busy.

"Boy . . ."

"Plus the cousins who just came, you met them last winter, and did you see my Aunt Rosalie and Uncle Mike?"

"A lot, huh?"

"Plus your parents and Georgie's parents and *my* parents . . ."

"I *am* getting nervous," she said, but smiled.

"Hey, Eddie!" Georgie sidled up to us. "Look over there."

"Where?"

"Heading toward the table."

I looked at the big picnic table where my mother

and Aunt Rosalie and Mrs. Redding and Mrs. Sunday were beginning to place the food platters. My father was nearby fussing with the barbecue.

"Look at what, Georgie?" Everything looked normal to me.

"Wait'll our parents move away, then you'll see . . . There! See? Who's that guy?"

I could see why Georgie asked. He was middle-aged, maybe around thirty-five, but he had on a checked sport jacket, an orange tie, and electric blue pants. He was helping himself to the food barely after it was put down.

"Is that one of your neighbors?" Ivy whispered.

"No, I never saw him before."

"You sure?"

"I'd remember *him,* wouldn't I?"

Ivy laughed. "For sure," she said. "Go ask who he is."

"Ask *him?*"

"*No,* ask your mother."

"Okay."

I caught Mom as she was heading back toward the house.

"Mom, hey, Mom, wait a minute . . ."

She turned impatiently. "I'm busy, Eddie, I've got to bring out the—"

"Just a second, Mom, who's that guy? The one with the—"

"Eddie! Don't point!" She took my hand. "It's not polite!"

"Well, who is he?" I jerked my head in his direction. "You know—the one with the—"

"Oh! Eddie! The salad!"

"The salad's out there."

"No, not the tuna salad. The potato salad. Would you get it, please? Come on, honey, I want everyone to eat and fill up so they're all happy when you play. Okay?" She disappeared into the house, reappeared almost immediately and handed me a red bowl.

"Ma, who—"

"Put it on the table. Next to the celery and olives. In back of the chopped liver. Go."

I went. She wasn't going to tell me.

"Well? Who is he?" Ivy asked, taking the bowl from me.

"I don't know. She wouldn't tell me."

"How come?" Georgie asked, and took the bowl from Ivy. "What am I doing with this bowl?"

"I don't know," I shrugged, took the bowl back and brought it to the table. They followed.

"Go ask your father," Ivy said. "We'll come with you."

"Ivy thinks he's someone special," Georgie explained.

"Okay . . ."

My father was sweating over the grill. My mother had bought him a white apron that had *Don't Bother Me, I'm Cooking* on it in big red letters. She also got him a white chef's hat to go with it which he'd finally consented to wear.

"Hey, Pop, who's that guy with the checked sport jacket and orange tie?"

My father said, "Don't bother me, I'm cooking."

"Couldn't you just tell us who he is, Mr. Levy?" Ivy asked.

"Yeah, who is he, Pop?"

"Ask your mother."

"I did. She wouldn't tell me."

"Ask her again." He began to poke around at the white-hot charcoal.

Ivy pulled Georgie and me away. "I told you. He's important. I bet he owns a big disco."

"We don't play disco," Georgie reminded her.

"So . . . he's a television producer."

"Do television producers dress like that?"

Ivy shrugged. "Eddie, if you don't know who he is, then he's gotta be somebody!"

I thought I knew what she meant.

Everybody ate a lot and seemed to be having a nice time. Uncle Mike was the bartender and he had special drinks for the kids. Ivy and I found that we really were too nervous to eat or drink much, but Georgie, who was supposed to be the nervous one, pigged out! Ivy and I were afraid he'd get sick before we played, but he didn't and kept on eating.

Finally, my mother clapped her hands.

"Everyone!" she called. "Everyone!"

My stomach felt weird. I went over to where the

11

instruments were and patted them, like they were puppies. I just didn't know what to do with my hands . . .

"Everyone! It's time for the entertainment!" my mother sang and the guests all started quieting down.

"Find a chair, everyone!" she called and everyone did.

"Hey," I whispered while the guests were grabbing chairs. "We'll start out with *The Saints,* okay?"

"I think *Free Bird,*" Georgie whispered back. "Let's *end* with *The Saints.*"

"No." Louder whisper from me. *"Free Bird* is too soft to open with!"

"Why didn't we figure this out before!" Ivy got in her own whisper, as my mother was saying, "It is my extreme pleasure and delight to present to you The Centerin City Blues Trio!"

"Listen, Eddie," Georgie said, "we should open with just the right—"

"Come on guys, they're getting quiet!" Ivy said loudly and since there was silence in the audience just at that point, everyone laughed at Ivy's stage-whisper warning.

Ivy rolled her eyes. "It's a good thing I'm black or would I be red!" she muttered. "Come on, Eddie, just call it. We'll play it."

I called *Sweet Georgia Brown* and we played it!

## 2.

We could play six songs: *When the Saints Go Marching In, Yellow Submarine, Sweet Georgia Brown, Free Bird, Alley Cat,* and a little thing I made up that we called *Eddie's Tune.* Our stuff was kind of a mixture of blues, soft rock and Dixie.

From the beginning, back in sixth grade, we had wanted to be different, different from all the other kid-groups you hear. Well, *I* had wanted to be different, anyway. I remember the day I brought Ivy and Georgie home to listen to my mother's Dukes of Dixieland and Billie Holiday records.

"Boy, Eddie, I never played that kind of music before," Georgie said. He was frowning.

"I know."

"I mean, it's not rock."

"Nope," I said.

"Don't you think we should play rock? Don't you, Ivy?" he asked.

"Listen," I told them. "You know the Screaming Eagles?"

"Zach Beecher's group?"

"Yeah. What do they play?"

"Rock."

13

"Right. And you know Laughing Moose?"

"That eighth grade band?"

"Yeah. What do they play?"

"Rock."

"Right. And you know the—"

"Okay, okay," Ivy interrupted. "Everybody and his uncle plays rock and you think we should be different, is that it, Eddie?"

"Right! See, we're good musicians! Aren't we? And we're going to be a great group! Aren't we going to be great?" They nodded solemnly. "We are! So combined with being really good musicians, if we pick a kind of music that isn't like everyone else's then we'll work more!"

Ivy nodded again. "I like rhythm-and-blues," she said. "I always have."

"Don't you like it, Georgie?" I asked. "It's not too complicated and we can improvise as we go along."

"I guess . . ."

But once we started playing together I didn't have to do any more persuading. We enjoyed the new songs and the sounds we were making and we practiced every chance we got.

I didn't think much about it then, but different can mean trouble. Most people—well, kids, anyway—are all into "the same." You have to be the same, do the same as everyone else, wear the same sneakers, jeans, jackets. Different isn't always terrific.

14

But the afternoon of the party, what did I know? I was happy! There we were, playing our music and being appreciated by an audience who had just given Georgie a big ovation after his solo.

I began to play again and as I did I looked up to see that the rest of the neighborhood had somehow appeared in our backyard. They were sitting on our fence and on the grass. Each person was clapping his hands and Cousin Audrey's husband Arthur had started everyone singing along. While everyone was cheering and clapping, my mother kissed all three of us, which was a little humiliating, but nice.

Afterward, it was like a blur. All the guests came up and congratulated us; Alice and Andrew started banging Ivy's drums and she had to take the sticks away and hide them. So Andrew kicked at the bass and Audrey sent him upstairs to my room. The uninvited neighbors got into the rest of the food and Uncle Mike got mobbed at the bar. My father, sweating buckets into his chief's hat, was grilling franks and burgers like one of those speeded-up silent movies. Aunt Rosalie sent me down to the corner for more ground round but when I came racing back, a lot of the people had left.

Ivy's father was helping load her drums into his grocery truck and Georgie was dragging his amp toward his parents' car. People were doing all those things they do when they're getting ready to leave someplace.

"Lovely, just lovely . . ."

"Thank you for having us, you have a talented son . . ."

"Great burgers, Norman . . ."

"Thank you so much, see you at . . ."

"Loved it, thank you . . ."

"Thank . . ."

Gone.

All except for Ivy and Georgie and Aunt Rosalie and Cousin Mike and the strange man in the checked sport jacket and orange tie, who was the only one sitting in a lawn chair, still with a big plate of food on his lap.

My mother said, "Eddie, you get Ivy and Georgie and come over here, there's someone I'd like you to meet."

"It's about time," I said and my mother said "Sh!"

The four of us stood around this eating rainbow in the lawn chair.

"Ivy, Eddie and Georgie," my mother said with a big grin, "I'd like to introduce you to Mr. Jack Dreiser!" She said it with a big flourish, the kind Ivy uses to end her drum solo. If the name was supposed to mean something to any of us, it didn't. We looked blankly at each other and then at Mr. Jack Dreiser.

"It's *Driver*," the man said.

"Oh. I'm so sorry . . ."

"Yeah, hi, kids," he said and dug into his potato salad.

16

We said, "Hi."

"Mr. Driver is with CBS Records," my mother said grandly.

Ivy tugged on my shirt. "I *told* you!" she whispered excitedly.

"Oh!" Georgie cried. "Really? CBS Records?"

Mr. Driver said, "Yep."

"Well," my mother said, backing away. "I'll leave you artists alone to talk."

"Well, gee," I said, wondering what was expected of me. Or Mr. Driver. Or any of us artists. "Gee, it was nice you could come, Mr. Driver," I said.

"Enjoyed it," he mumbled through the potato salad. "Great potato salad."

I looked at Ivy and Georgie who were looking at me.

"Are you a friend of my mother's?" I asked lamely. I somehow felt it was up to me to keep some kind of artistic conversation going.

"Nope," he said. "Just met her today. Nice lady. Gives a nice barbecue."

I said, "Yeah, I guess so . . ."

"What did you think of our playing, Mr. Driver?" Ivy asked right out, the way I never would have.

"Mm?"

"Our *group.* Our *trio.* Our *music,*" Ivy said. Georgie shook his head and rolled his eyes.

"Yeah, the music," Mr. Driver said and swallowed. "Well. You kids are pretty good musicians."

We looked at each other and grinned.

"How old are you, 'leven? Twelve?"

We nodded, still with those silly grins on our faces.

"Yeah. Well. You play pretty good. You all studying?"

Ivy and Georgie both nodded.

"Not you?" Mr. Driver said, looking at me.

"Uh, no, I couldn't find the right teacher . . ."

"Not surprised, not surprised," Mr. Driver mumbled. "Hard to teach a kid with your kind of (mumble). Say, you got any of this potato salad left?"

My mother would have killed me if she'd known, but I ignored his request. "What did you say, sir?" I asked. "Hard to teach a kid with my kind of—what?"

"Oh. Yeah. I got a teacher for you. He's great. Lives over in Jefferson. Bit of a hike, but worth it. Ham Carpenter. Hamilton Carpenter. Got a pencil, kid?"

"Well, but Mr. Driver, how about our—"

"Never mind, got one here someplace . . ." He put his paper plate down on the grass and stood up, poking around in his pockets.

"We used to work together," he said, "over at CBS, but Ham gave it all up for—" He found a pencil stub, ripped a piece off his paper plate and wrote. We made disgusted faces at each other while he was writing.

"Here," he said, handing me the edge of his

18

plate. "Listen, thanks. Nice meeting you. Your folks throw a great barbecue." And he was gone.

We sat down on the grass, not looking at each other this time and not even speaking. My mother was instantly upon us.

"I thought he'd say goodbye," she said. "He didn't come in to say goodbye."

"He said goodbye," I muttered. "He said you throw a great barbecue."

"What's wrong? Didn't he like you? Everybody liked you!"

I handed her the piece of paper plate.

"What's this?"

"It's the name of a piano teacher for me. He lives in Jefferson. If that guy was a talent scout, Ma, he sure didn't act like he saw any talent."

Georgie asked, "How'd you get him here, Mrs. Levy?"

"Well, my friend, Arlene, you know Arlene, Eddie—"

I nodded impatiently. I'd only known Arlene since I was born.

"Well, Arlene has this next-door neighbor whose cousin has a brother who works for this law firm in New York City."

I sighed. "So?"

"Well, this law firm does some work for CBS, some part of it, anyway . . ."

"Yeah?"

"And one of the people in the firm became

friendly with a man connected in some way, I forget which, with CBS records."

"And Mr. Driver was the man?"

"No, no," my mother said and I laughed out loud. "No, Mr. Driver was the friend. The friend of the man who's connected with CBS records who knows the person in the law firm who knows the brother of Arlene's next-door neighbor's cousin!"

Ivy, Georgie and I burst out laughing and my mother did, too.

"Well, it was complicated, but I wanted somebody important to listen to you kids," my mother said.

"Thanks, Ma," I said and meant it. "Thanks for the confidence."

"At least *someone* has confidence in us, Mrs. Levy," Georgie mumbled.

"Wait a minute," I said. "He did say we were good musicians."

"Aw," Georgie said, "that was probably just talk. He had to say something, he was eating all your potato salad . . ."

"Oh, Georgie, come on!" Ivy said. "The neighbors liked us. And Mr. Driver thinks you should study, Eddie. Maybe we're not good enough yet for a real talent scout . . ."

"Well, he's not exactly a talent scout," my mother said and coughed. "So what does he know, anyway?"

"What do you mean?" I asked. "Isn't he a talent scout? He's from CBS Records, isn't he? Ma?"

"Well, yes, he's from CBS Records . . . He's a copyright lawyer. He's in their legal department."

"I don't get it. He's a lawyer? Not a talent scout?"

My mother raised her arms. "He's from CBS Records, right? He knows people to talk to, right? And anyway—" she put her arms down with a sheepish smile—"he was the only one I could get."

I shook my head. "Listen, Ma," I said, "let's call the teacher."

❀

It wasn't that we hadn't tried to find a teacher for me before.

Back in the fourth grade when I was nine, I walked over to our rinky-dink upright piano one day and plunked out the old Beatles tune, *Yellow Submarine*. With one finger, of course.

You would've thought I'd discovered oil in our backyard, the way my mother carried on. "A musical genius! In our very own family! He gets it from my sister, Rosalie, remember how beautifully she used to play the harmonica!"

My father listened to my mother and nodded his head.

"Nice, Eddie," he said to me.

Now that I look back on it, what I did was no big deal. *Yellow Submarine* is practically all one note. Da da da da-da dum de dum de dum . . . Nothing to it.

But my mother thought she was raising another

Ludwig Von. She got on the phone immediately and somehow conjured up Amelie Nordenhof, who was visiting our neighbors, the Cranmers, from somewhere in Sweden or Austria or Germany or Norway. Amelie Nordenhof, it seems, was an accomplished pianist in whatever country she lived, and lucky us, she was willing to give me piano lessons once a week or even twice if I showed half the promise my mother said I did.

If I showed any promise, I sure didn't show it to Amelie Nordenhof, who burst into tears after three lessons and told me a lot of things in her native language which fortunately I didn't understand.

We all thought that was the end of my piano lessons, but my mother persisted.

Somehow through my cousin Morton, the one who goes to Dartmouth, she found Herbie Purvis who Morton grew up with when he and my Aunt and Uncle used to live here in Centerin City. Herbie Purvis, Morton said, played pop and jazz and rock, went to Centerin City Community College (better known as See-See-See-See and very rough to say if you have a lisp), and gave piano lessons. He gave two months' worth to me.

I guess he played all right himself, and he did teach me how to read notes and play chords, but he whined at me all the time. If I made a mistake or I didn't play the song exactly the way he wanted me to, he whined. He called me "Ed-deeee" and shook his glasses at me while he held them by the stem. He also was partial to stride piano—where you bounce your left hand all over the place playing ragtime or Dixie—which I liked a lot and was glad to learn, but I wanted to do it other ways, too. The trouble with Herbie was he wouldn't listen to any of my ideas, he kept saying to learn it all the right way first and that turned me off because I wasn't too sure his way *was* the right way. He kept reminding me I was only nine, which bugged me, because I couldn't see what my age had to do with the musical ideas I wanted to try out. Toward the end of what turned out to be my last lesson, I played something differently and Herbie shook his glasses at me and said, "No, no, no, no, no!" I responded by saying, "Rats, rats, rats, rats, rats!" and that was my last encounter with Herbie Purvis.

The next teacher my mother got through my sister Yvonne's ballet school. She was a nice lady named Ms. Duffy and she played the accompaniment for the ballet school's lessons and recitals. She never put me down for trying to do things differently from the way the notes on the page said you should play them, but I think she was a little confused by me. Besides that, she had some problems. She broke up with some guy that she still liked, I guess, because all through my lessons, she kept listening for the phone to ring. I found that out because I finally asked her why she kept leaning back on the piano bench with her eyes glazed over and her head kind of cocked to one side. She burst into tears and confided to me between sobs that she was waiting for this phone call she was sure was going to come through at any time and who it would be and what he did for a living and a whole lot of other stuff I didn't really want to know.

So Ms. Duffy and I just drifted apart after that, though I can still see her on the piano bench, tilted toward the kitchen, with her hair hanging out in back of her, perpendicular to the floor. Sometimes I wonder if that relationship ever did work out, but I'd bet against it.

It was after Ms. Duffy that we decided to give up on piano teachers. Not that my mother and I are easy giver-uppers. I guess both of us drive my father kind of crazy with our singlemindedness. The time I was playing Dungeons and Dragons with two kids from my class and two from down the street, all my family heard for months were character names, possessions, treasures, hit points, armor class and spells.

And my mother—her singlemindedness mostly involves me and my sister, Yvonne.

My family is really perfect for me, because while my mother thinks I'm practically the Coming of the Messiah, my father counters her enthusiasm by nodding and saying "That's nice" a lot when you know he's not even listening. So between the two of them, I've learned to be a fair judge of my own abilities. My mother is a pretty good ego booster— I mean, she thinks my sister Yvonne is ready to join the American Ballet Company, and you just have to see my sister Yvonne up on her toes to know that's a little far from the truth—but it's nice when someone thinks you're pretty perfect.

The reason we gave up on piano teachers was because I was beginning to take off on my own. I was picking out songs with both hands and could play things I liked on the radio by ear, mostly Beatles tunes, some Elton John, stuff like that.

Playing piano is—I guess—my favorite thing to do. I discovered that back in fourth grade, the same year I discovered Ivy Sunday, my favorite person.

Fourth grade is when they start giving free music lessons in school. All you pay is the rental of the instrument. Piano wasn't one of the instruments offered, but percussion was, and Ivy started taking drum lessons then.

She told me she'd been playing long before that, even before she turned two years old, with the sticks from a little tin drum her brother gave her. She didn't use the drum, but she used the sticks— on the radiator, on the furniture, on her father's leg, on the truck dashboard. She says she played drums before she could walk or talk.

She was in my class then. But I didn't pay much attention to her, or she to me, until I saw her play drums in the fourth-grade band concert. She stood

25

out like a diamond in a pile of rocks. There were all these little kids—well, I was, too, but anyway, there they were tooting and hooting and huffing and puffing, squeaking and wailing, honking, groaning, and all of them with red and sweaty faces . . . I know it's not nice to say, but I wanted to take my shirt off and stuff it into my ears. I mean, they were trying hard and everything, I appreciated that, but those noises would've sent Canadian geese back to Toronto.

But Ivy—she was something else. She had a solo. She had to have a solo, she was the prime mover and shaker—she was the shining light of the whole school: this small little girl, grinning away, not caring who was there or where they were or where *she* was, just hittin' those skins and tappin' that cymbal, feet moving, every inch of her a real loving musician. She had her hair in those short little corn rows and they were all moving with each bob of her head! She just looked wonderful!

I remember going home that night and thinking: If I ever get my own group together, I want that girl to play drums in it!

But I never said that to Ivy. At least not back then in fourth grade. What I said to her when I saw her the next day in school was: "Hey, that was nice. Your solo."

She grinned. She said, "Thanks."

"Where you take?" I asked her.

"Here," she said. "School."

"You learned to play drums like that in school?"

I asked. "How come the horn players didn't learn as well as you did?"

"Because I have talent," she said.

Well, of course, she was right, it was a stupid question. I guess I was thinking of my times with Amelie Nordenhof and Herbie Purvis and Ms. Duffy—and thinking I have talent, too. Despite my teacher experiences.

Anyway, those were the only words I spoke to Ivy in fourth grade.

In fifth grade, she played in the band concert again and I went just to hear her. Once again she was great and the horns were all sour.

Afterwards, I went backstage and told her how much I liked her playing.

"Yeah, I remember you," she said and smiled. "You said that last year. I keep track of all my compliments."

I grinned back at her.

"Well, thanks again. You play an instrument?" she asked.

"Yeah, piano."

"Piano, huh?" She looked over toward a back corner of the stage. I followed her gaze and saw an old upright pushed against the wall with the bench, minus two legs, sitting on top. She tilted her head in that direction and said, "Come on."

I dragged a chair over to the piano and played a few chords. The piano wasn't too out of tune, but some of the keys were stuck. Anyhow, it didn't matter, because once we got into *Sweet Georgia*

*Brown* with Ivy beating along on the side of the piano, smiling like crazy, I forgot everything and played *Georgia* like I'd never played it before! When we finished the final chorus, Ivy gave me an even wider grin, stuck out her hand and said, "It's nice to meet another musician. Say, what's your name, anyway?"

I thought again that it'd be fun for us to work together, but I still didn't say anything. Then in sixth grade, Ivy heard a new kid—Georgie Redding—audition for something. He played Lynyrd Skynard's *Free Bird* on his guitar and sang it, and Ivy introduced him to me and we played for each other. Georgie had wiry red hair and freckles all over his face and arms and when he wailed on his axe—that's what he called his guitar—I could have sworn all those freckles bounced around, too, like sixteenth notes!

That was it. I don't remember the first one of us to suggest forming a group, though it was probably me. But I still like to think that it was Fate or Destiny that brought us together because the three of us were so *right* together.

The night of our barbeque which was such a big hit with Mr. Driver, the night of our trio's first public appearance which was such a big hit with the neighbors and our families, Ma called Hamilton Carpenter.

She didn't have to persist. He was home and he was interested right from the start.

## 3.

Hamilton Carpenter's walk-up "studio"—a one-room apartment with one piano, one couch, one table, no sunlight, no rugs, and a part-time cat—was about forty minutes away from our house in Centerin City. Hamilton Carpenter himself was about thirty, maybe thirty-five—the same age as Mr. Driver, maybe, only Mr. Driver was a lot older, if you know what I mean.

For our first interview, he had decked himself out in an undershirt and painter's pants. He had a salt-and-pepper beard and mustache, but not much hair on top. He smiled a lot. I liked him. My mother looked like she wanted to clean his apartment while he and I were talking, so I managed to sit her down on the couch real quick and I sat next to her.

Ham told us he used to be a lawyer and chucked it all because what he always should have been was a musician. He said he didn't even learn to read notes until he was in his late twenties because everything he played was by ear. Then he sat down at the piano and played for us and just about knocked my socks off.

First he played *Twinkle, Twinkle, Little Star*. No, I'm not kidding, that's what he played, and he played it just like the Walt Disney movies and you could practically see Tinker Bell float across the room. Then, when I was wondering just what the heck this was all about, he launched into *Twinkle, Twinkle* in a classical style. Like Mozart was playing or something. And before I latched onto that, he was playing *Twinkle, Twinkle* in a raunchy blues style, then a jazz style, then a ragtime style. I couldn't believe it, it was so terrific! Even my mother was tapping her foot the whole time.

"See, Eddie," he said when he was finished, "the notes are only somebody else's opinion. You should know how to read them, of course, but they're not the last word. As a musician, you should make your own contribution to the song."

I was in heaven. It was what I had tried to tell Amelie Nordenhof and Herbie Purvis and even Ms. Duffy, only I didn't know how and they didn't care.

So I started to study with Ham.

Ivy called the night of my first lesson.

"How was it?" she asked, sounding excited.

"It was great, really great. He's terrific, you should have heard what he did with *Twinkle, Twinkle, Little Star!*"

There was a pause. *"Twinkle, Twinkle, Little Star?"*

Ivy asked, wrinkling her nose. I couldn't see her, but I could tell her nose was wrinkled.

"No, it was just an example, Ivy. I mean all the different ways you can play one song and make it brand new each time, *Twinkle* was just like an exercise, that's all."

"Oh," she said, laughing. "I knew you wanted us to be different, Eddie, but nursery rhymes are a little too different for even me."

"Don't worry. I'm going to learn a lot from this guy."

"Oh, good, that's just what we need! I expect great things from you, Eddie. Do you have something for us to work on tomorrow at Georgie's?"

*"Tomorrow?* Hey, I just started! But I guess I could do *Twink—*"

"Forget it. See you at rehearsal!"

"Bye, Ivy. And thanks for calling . . ."

My mother never complained about the long drive to Ham's place. Twice a week she'd get us into the car—my sister Yvonne and her ballet tights and slippers and toe shoes, and me, with my notebooks and sheet music. She'd drop Yvonne off at the Centerin City Dance Academy and then haul me on to Jefferson, where she'd wait downstairs in the car reading a *People* magazine, while I stayed upstairs watching my whole life begin.

Ham taught me how to play the melody notes on

top of the chords in the right hand, not the left like most people do it, and how to do a walking bass line in the left hand. Eventually he taught me theory, but it was painless and kind of sneaked into the lessons. He said I was a natural player and picked up quicker than anyone he ever taught!

I was so excited that that's when I told him about the band. I thought if he could just hear us practice, he'd give us an opinion I could really respect.

"Sure, Eddie," he said. "Sure, I'll come over and hear you wail."

He was in Georgie's basement two days later. We were nervous, but we tried to play just the way we'd played at the party. We did three tunes and made sure each of us had a solo.

Ham listened and smiled and nodded. When we were finished, he said, "Well, you guys are pretty good musicians."

"That's what Mr. Driver said," Georgie muttered, frowning. "And we don't even have any potato salad!"

"Do you *really* think we're good?" I asked.

Ham leaned forward. "Yeah," he said, "I really do. I think you're all excellent. But I know what your trouble is."

"What?" Ivy asked without looking at him.

"Well, now, what was that stuff you were playing there? Uh, *Yellow Submarine, Georgia Brown, The Saints* . . . right?"

"Right," Georgie said.

"See . . . those songs are good and not usually what you'd hear kids play and that's fine. Only—well—the instrumentation is wrong, you know what I mean?"

Ivy said, "No."

"See, what you've got to do, you've got to figure out what sound you want and what instruments you need for that sound. You wouldn't play a Beethoven concerto with a bunch of harmonicas, would you?"

We shook our heads.

"Well, do you want a rock sound, a Dixie sound . . . or what?"

"We want to sound like a blues band," I said.

"Yeah, and we want to be able to improvise," Ivy said.

"Not real fast stuff," Georgie said, "not real complicated . . . Like Ivy said, we want to create as we go along."

"And we have electric instruments," I added.

"Okay, okay." Ham leaned forward again and touched his fingertips together. "Sounds like you want the kind of stuff the Butterfield Blues Band did around the late sixties. Or The Blues Project. Maybe Eric Clapton. But what you've got to get—you've got to get a bass, you definitely need a bass guitar, and you should get yourselves a horn."

"A *horn?*"

"Sure, absolutely. You remember Blood, Sweat and Tears? They were the first rock band with horns."

I looked at Ivy. "You know anyone who plays a horn?"

"What kind of horn?" Ivy asked Ham.

"Well, trumpet, trombone . . ."

Ivy shook her head. "No one who's really any good, anyway . . ."

"If you can only get one horn, make it a trumpet," Ham said. He looked at our faces. "You're not discouraged, are you? Come on, you're really excellent players, you just need to get yourself a sound. Listen to some records. Listen to Chicago, Yard Birds. Hey, it takes time to develop a sound, y'know?"

✢

"A sound," I said, almost to myself when Ham had left. "Well, he's right . . ."

"Yeah, he is right," Ivy said. "And with a bass and horn, boy, nobody is going to sound like us! We'll be outa sight!"

"Mmmmmmmmm," Mrs. Redding said. Or coughed. Or hummed. She'd been sitting on the basement stairs, listening to us play for Ham.

"What's the matter, Mom?" Georgie said, knowing what the matter was.

"Georgie, the tiles—"

"I know, I know, they're bouncing off the

34

kitchen walls. Listen, why don't we just *paint* the kitchen?"

Mrs. Redding got up and came all the way downstairs.

"Georgie, it isn't funny. I hate to be the one to put a damper on things but I'm finding it harder and harder to take the noise. All right, sound. Music. Whatever. The floor shakes and I'm getting headaches. Now if you're going to add more instruments, especially a *horn*, well, I'm really sorry, but you're going to have to look around for a practice place."

"Come on, Mom," Georgie began, but she put up her hand.

"Georgie, I mean it. I *am* sorry—Eddie, Ivy—I think your teacher's right, you are good musicians. Georgie, I've always encouraged you, gave you lessons—"

"Come on, Mom," Georgie said again. I was thinking maybe Georgie could find some new words—or at least more interesting ones,—but he could only manage "Come on, Mom" and of course, Ivy and I couldn't say anything . . .

Georgie's mother sighed. "Well . . ." she said, shrugging. "I don't want you to have to give up on your band . . . But please, try to find someplace else if you can?"

I slammed the screen door loudly by accident and didn't realize I'd startled my father who had just come home and had settled down in his chair to relax.

"Sorry," I said.

"A simple 'hello' next time would be nice," he said, rearranging himself in the chair.

"The door slipped. I was thinking," I said.

"Thinking. What's to think about at your age? Get to my age, then you *think.*"

"Aw, you're not that old, Pop. There's a lot to think about at my age, too. Don't you remember?"

"I don't remember *yesterday,*" he snorted. "So tell me. What's the big think?"

"Well, Ham came to our practice session today and he made a lot of suggestions. You know, about like the way for us to develop the right sound. The kind of music we should be playing and the kind of instrumentation we need . . ."

My father grunted. "What's wrong with the music you've been doing?"

"The stuff we've been doing is a mish-mash of styles. Ham thinks the kind of thing we want is a lot like the blues they used to play in the late sixties. Not a jumble of the thirties and the eighties."

My father raised his eyebrows.

"Don't you remember any of that sixties stuff, Pop?"

"Eddie, who had time to listen to music? I've been working since I was fourteen. Going to school at night, starting my business, I didn't even have time to get married before I got bald!"

I sighed. "Well, anyway . . . we have to find a bass. And a horn."

Another grunt.

"Ham's right," I continued, "it sounds like what we've been aiming for . . . but now we have a real direction."

"Well, he's a teacher. He ought to know what he's talking about."

I let my breath out. "Yeah . . ."

My father sank back in his chair. "So why don't you call your cousin Audrey?" he said.

"Audrey?"

"Audrey, yes. She was one of those run-arounds in the sixties, Audrey was."

"Run-arounds?"

"Run-arounds, you know, hippies, beatniks, whatever name they called the kids, don't ask me, Eddie, but she played music all the time. Always music, drove Rosalie crazy, like you're driving me."

"I drive you crazy, Pop?"

He smiled at me and shook his head. "Go call up Audrey, maybe she knows the music you want to listen to."

I beamed. "Thanks, Pop, that's a good idea!"

It was. Audrey had Blood, Sweat and Tears and Eric Clapton and some other stuff that Ham had mentioned and she promised to make cassettes for me.

"Tell Audrey hello!" my mother called to me and I was so excited I nearly asked her to drive me to

Riverdale but forced myself to have patience till Audrey could mail the tapes. I couldn't wait to tell Ivy and Georgie!

❀

"How much have you got?" I asked.

"Four dollars," Ivy said. "It's absolutely all I can spare."

"I've got two-fifty," Georgie said. "In change."

"That's okay, it's still money. I've got five dollars and thirty-seven cents. How many tapes can we get for that?"

"Are you kidding? Only one, Eddie," Georgie said.

"All right, look, then we'll get one. And we'll listen to it all afternoon. And in a few days we'll have a lot of stuff from Audrey and we'll have a real good idea of what we want when we're ready to add the new kids."

"Yeah . . . the new kids," Ivy said. "Gee, we found each other so perfectly, I hope we'll find two more who fit in so well."

"Yeah . . ."

"And how *are* we going to find them?" Georgie asked. "Walk down Latham Avenue and stop anyone carrying an instrument case?"

"No. I know how we should do it," Ivy said with a little smile. "I thought about it all last night. What I think we should do is have an open audition!"

"Hey!" I cried. "That sounds like a great idea!"

"What we should do," Ivy continued, "is print up flyers. Maybe your father could do it, Eddie, through his company. And then we could post the flyers all over town, announcing the date and the place and everything."

"That's terrific!" I cried. "They could say: 'In these days of rampant inflation, the Centerin City Blues Trio is now hiring two more players.'"

"Right!" Ivy said. "We're expanding to give kids more jobs. Big business should follow our example."

"Yeah. And we'll make the words 'horn' and 'bass' in big letters," Georgie said. "Maybe we should say something about age."

"Age?"

"Well, yeah, I mean, what if we get some sixteen-year-old kids or something."

I thought about it. "Would that be bad?" I asked. "Maybe their experience would help."

"Naw, older kids would boss us around," Georgie said.

"Maybe you're right . . ."

"Sure. Think about it. Pretty soon they'd be telling us what to do and what to play and everything. Older kids are like that. I ought to know, I've got two younger brothers."

"Do you boss Yvonne around, Eddie?" Ivy asked.

"Well . . . I would if I could, but she doesn't listen to me," I admitted. "Does Raymond boss you around, Ivy?"

"Sure," she grumbled.

"And we already decided on the music we want to play. If an older kid doesn't like it then pretty soon we'll be playing *his* stuff. Older and younger kids. It's a way of life," Georgie sighed.

"Okay, what should we say then? Only twelve- or thirteen-year-olds?" I asked.

Ivy suggested, "What about saying 'under fourteen'?"

Georgie nodded. "I guess that'd be okay. Even if we get a fourteen-year-old, that's close enough to thirteen and twelve to not get too bossy." It sounded logical . . .

"Good," I said. "We're all set."

"No, we're not," Georgie said.

"Georgie, the Prophet of Gloom!" Ivy wailed. "Now what?"

"Well, with my mother's tiles dropping off the walls, where are we going to rehearse?"

"Don't worry," I said. "My mother will think of something."

❈

She did.

"You can use the garage, Eddie," she said, "if you clean it out. It's so full of junk we can't get the car in there anyway, so you might as well take it."

Good old Ma! We got busy right away. We took all the junk from the inside of the garage and piled it up in the back, on the *outside* of it. Unfortunately that wasn't what my mother had in mind, so we took an extra day hauling it down to the junk yard on Skilman Avenue. My father got our flyers printed up, and we found a big padlock for the garage doors. Once we were all through, it was great! We were ready!

It was just mid-August, and since Labor Day was late we figured that if we had the audition right away, we'd get our musicians and we'd have a whole lot of good practicing time before school got in the way.

So we made the audition for the very next Sunday. We thought that way we'd get the kids who worked who wouldn't be able to come during the week.

We flew around the neighborhood for two days tacking up flyers wherever anyone said it wasn't illegal and even in places where it was. I thought the flyers looked great. They had black lettering on tan paper and they said:

ALL YOU GREAT MUSICIANS
WITH NO PLACE TO CALL HOME

The Centerin City Blues Trio is expanding!

Bring your Bass Guitar or Horn (trumpets preferred) to an audition at 24 Coral Place at 1:00 P.M. on Sunday, August 18th.
(Don't ring the bell, go into the garage.)

*Over fourteen need not apply.*

The rest of our time that week was taken up listening to all the blues music we could: Audrey's tapes and our tape and some old records of Ham's and not only did we love it, we really couldn't wait to play it!

I hoped that my parents wouldn't mind that the place would be mobbed. The Saturday night before I had a dream that the garage was so full of kids and horns and bass guitars that it bulged out at the seams and the neighbors were so upset about the noise and crowds that they called the police and my father came out to quiet everyone down wearing a big apron that read *Don't Bother Me, I'm Cooking,* and my mother smiled and smiled and said, "It's all right, they're so talented."

I woke up in a sweat and then I relaxed. I think I got Georgie's dream by mistake.

Sunday morning, Ivy came over with a tape recorder and some cardboard signs in the shape of arrows that had *This way to the audition* painted on them in magic marker.

"We're going to put these signs up on Garvey and Coral, too," she said, "like they do with detours, to help people find your house. Come on, help me." Excitedly we ran out to place the signs while my mother made lunch for us. Georgie came over at about a quarter to one, just as we were finishing.

"Hey, I saw the signs," he said. "That was a good idea, I was worried about how the people would find us."

"Don't worry, Georgie, they'll find us," Ivy said.

"Is there going to be enough room in there?" he asked. "What if we're mobbed or something, what if we can't handle it, will the people have to wait outside, or what?"

"Georgie—"

"I know, why don't I stand outside and direct everybody?"

I shrugged. "Okay. Ivy and I'll stay in the garage."

"You and Ivy stay in the garage," Georgie said.

"Aw, come on, Georgie, calm down," Ivy said. "It'll be all right. It'll be fun."

"Right, okay," he said hesitantly.

"Can I watch?" my sister Yvonne begged.

"Why don't you help Georgie direct the traffic to the garage?" I suggested. "You could stand at one end of the block and Georgie could stay at the other."

"You think there'll be a lot of people?" she asked.

"Mobs," I said.

"Okay, I'll direct traffic!" and she bounced out with Georgie, while Ivy and I went out the back to the garage.

"Any minute now," I said excitedly as we sat on the stools we had brought out earlier.

"We're going to be a band!" she cried happily.

"I wish Georgie would quit worrying over everything, it's going to be fun."

Ivy smiled. "Poor Georgie. He reminds me of my grandmother. She has one word for every situation."

"What is it?"

"(Sigh)."

"Yeah, Georgie sighs a lot. I like . . . Georgie . . ."

"Oh, me too," Ivy said.

"I mean, I like him a lot and he's a good guitar player. But . . ."

"What?"

I chickened out. "Nothing," I said.

"No, what, Eddie?"

"Well . . . don't you think there's a special kind of wave length—you know, between the two of us?"

"Well . . . I guess." She smiled and looked at her shoe.

"There is, Ivy." I felt better about talking now. "We both feel the same way about things—music, the band, the way to do things—special friends, you know? The way special friends hit it off?"

"Yeah, I know, Eddie."

"Well, it's nice, that's all," I said.

"It is nice," she said. "Lots of kids have friends, but not all of them are special. Where you think alike." She nodded. "It's nice."

At one-thirty, Georgie came in.

"Where is everybody?" he asked, frowning. "Do you think they got lost? Do you think they had trouble finding the house?"

"Not even one person came to the corner so far?" I asked. "Not even one?"

"The only person to come down this block in the last half hour was a lady about a hundred-and-four years old walking a German Shepherd."

"Oh, yeah, that's Mrs. Gonzola."

"She wasn't carrying a horn, was she?" Ivy asked.

Georgie sat down heavily on the third stool. "Boy, I thought we'd really be mobbed, y'know?"

"I did, too! Everybody wants to play in a band! . . . Right?"

"Yeah, everybody . . ."

"Hey!"

We looked up. Someone was rapping on the side of the garage and staring at us. It was a boy, maybe around ten years old.

"Is this where you're supposed to try out?" he asked.

"Yeah," I said, getting off my stool. "Yeah! This is where! What've you got?"

"My horn," he said, coming toward us and holding it up.

"What *is* that?" Georgie whispered to Ivy.

"It's a bugle," she whispered. And then out loud to the kid: "What's your name?"

"Harvey Macomb. Should I play now?"

This was too much. "Yeah," I answered, "play, Harvey."

He played taps.

Then he played Flag Raising.

He stood at attention the whole time.

"Nice, Harvey," I said when he was finished. I thought I sounded like my father. "Very nice."

"Thanks, Harvey," Ivy said.

"Don't call us, we'll call you," Georgie said as Harvey and his bugle, complete with red, white and blue satin cord attached, left our garage forever.

"That's it?" Georgie asked the wall. "That's our whole terrific audition? What'll we *do?*"

"We'll wait," I said. "It's only two o'clock. We're bound to get some more people. "Let's listen to some of our best blues numbers. That'll cheer us up and give us ideas, too."

I went inside and brought out a Blood, Sweat and Tears tape and one of Eric Clapton's album "Layla." I put the first on the recorder Ivy had brought to tape the people who auditioned so we'd remember them.

"Oh, yeah!" Georgie said after the first cut. "I really like that trumpet solo in *Spinning Wheel.*"

"Yeah, and remember this?" I located *Layla* and turned it up loud.

We were moving and bopping around the garage to the rhythm when someone else came in. I turned off the tape.

"You like that?" I asked, grinning at the kid who was standing there.

"Isn't that great?" Ivy said. "It's just what your teacher meant about getting a special sound, Eddie."

"I'd be happy with *that* one," Georgie said, tapping the tape.

"Oh," the new kid sighed. "I knew it was dumb to come here."

"Why?"

"That music you were just playing. That's what you want, isn't it?"

"Oh, boy, it sure is." I grinned.

"It's not rock is it? And it sure isn't disco . . ."

"No, it's not. It's more like blues. Did you come to audition?"

"Well, yes and no," the kid said. "I don't have

anything you can use. I just wanted a chance to play for a new audience."

"But where's your instrument?" Ivy asked. "What do you play?"

"You're not going to believe this . . ."

*"What?"*

"Bagpipe," the kid said softly.

"Bagpipe?" That was the three of us.

"Yeah, I left it outside. I didn't want to see your instant reaction if I walked in with it."

"I can see why," I muttered.

"We said bass and horn on the flyer," Ivy said.

"Well . . . it's *like* a horn," the kid said. ". . . You blow into it . . ."

"We can't use a bagpipe, kid," I said.

"I know that, I know that. But look, how about if you just let me play for you, okay? I'm really good . . ."

"I'm sure you're good, but—"

"Come on, please? You don't know what it's like. With your instruments, you can play anywhere, anytime. The only time I ever get heard is in the Memorial Day Parade!"

"Sure, kid, go get it and play," I said.

He brought it in and played for us. Actually, he *was* good. And the music was nice. We couldn't use it, but it was nice. I guess I'd feel bad, too, if I only got to play once a year for an audience.

The kid was just finishing when another boy walked in.

48

"Okay, now we're rolling," Georgie whispered excitedly and Ivy muttered, "How come there aren't any girls?"

This new kid was tough-looking. He glowered at the kid with the bagpipe.

"You gotta be kidding," he said. "This the kind of band you got? What else is there, fife and drum?"

The kid with the bagpipe sighed. "Don't worry," he said. "I just came in to play for an audience for a few minutes."

"He only gets an audience on Memorial Day," I explained. I looked at the new kid. He had a black T-shirt with a red skull on it and he had rolled its sleeves practically up to his neck. He was also wearing a blue bandanna tied around his head and he had long, stringy brown hair sticking out from under it. He had a nylon satchel strapped to his back and he was carrying a guitar.

"You're a bass player," Ivy said, smiling as she got up from the floor.

"No, this here's a violin and I'm Henny Young-man," he said sarcastically. I started to hope he was terrible, so we wouldn't have to worry about using him.

"Okay," I said, "Let's see your stuff."

"Rat own," he drawled. "You ain't never seen nothin' like GROVER!"

Grover?

He put down his satchel and started to take

things out of it, which he began to stuff in his pockets and down his belt and in his bandanna.

Georgie and Ivy and I looked at each other.

Then he plugged in his bass, tuned up a little, and started to sing. No, not sing. It was more like screaming. No, maybe wailing. Maybe a combination of both. Scrailing?

We were just staring at him with our mouths open while he went on banging and screaming and then we jumped out of our skins. He started to pull out whatever it was he had hidden in his clothes and smash them onto the garage floor where they exploded like firecrackers. They smoked, too, and I hope to tell you, I was one scared piano player! Ivy let out a shriek every time one of those exploding things hit the floor and Georgie, who was closest to him, kept dancing out of the way.

"YAH!" Grover screamed and smashed a firecracker. I have to admit, every one was on the beat of the song.

"What is going on in here?"

I looked up to see our next-door neighbor, Mr. Broigen, standing there just inside the garage door. Grover and the firecrackers and the music stopped.

"Hello, Mr. Broigen," I said. "Did the noise, uh, sound . . . bother you?"

"*Doctor* Broigen," he corrected, "and yes, it most

certainly did. You know this garage is even closer to my house than to yours, Eddie."

"Sorry, sir," was all I could manage. I looked at Ivy and Georgie, who were kind of standing around making believe they weren't there. Only Grover was following the exchange between Mr.— *Dr.* Broigen and me.

"You say you're sorry, Eddie, but perhaps you don't know what you're sorry for."

"I'm sorry you were bothered, Dr. Broigen," I said out loud, and now please go home—to myself.

"You know, Eddie, I'm not some eccentric who sits at home all day spying on his neighbors."

Could've fooled me . . .

"No, I happen to be doing some very important, very exciting, very crucial work."

"Yes, sir, I'm sure," I said, just as another figure appeared next to him. It was my father in his Bermuda shorts and flowered Hawaiian shirt. I didn't know whether I was glad or sorry to see him.

"Mr. Levy," Dr. Broigen said. "I cannot have firecrackers and screaming children carrying on practically in my living room. I'd like to know what you're going to do about it."

My father looked at me. "Eddie. What are you going to do about it? And what's *that?*"

"Uh, that's Grover, Pop," I explained. "His work is, uh, accented."

"Accented?"

"Yeah, but it's okay, he's finished. He was just leaving. Thanks, Grover," I said.

"Don't you dig it?" Grover growled, zipping up his guitar case.

"Yeah. Yeah, we dig it. But we have a lot of other people to hear," I said.

"Right," he answered. "So I see." And he stalked out, brushing Dr. Broigen on the shoulder.

Dr. Broigen said, "Well!" and my father looked at him. "Mr. Levy, do you know what endothia parasitica is?"

My father said he didn't.

"It is a blight," Dr. Broigen explained. He said "ay" instead of "uh." "Ay chestnut-tree blight. Unless it is checked, it will destroy every chestnut tree in the northeast."

I said, "They were only firecrackers!" but nobody paid any attention.

Dr. Broigen went on. "If you care at all about preserving one of our more cherished forms of nature, you will understand how important it is that I be allowed to continue my work in peace and quiet."

My father was nodding his head slowly back and forth, but that didn't mean he was agreeing with Dr. Broigen, it was just something my father did a lot.

"You understand," Dr. Broigen said, and my father kept nodding.

"You're making a vaccine," I offered. "Like Dr. Salk. To make the tree better."

Dr. Broigen now directed his attention at me. "Not exactly," he said. "Some of us are trying to develop a more resistant kind of tree."

Ivy said, "That's nice," and I had to bite the inside of my cheek to keep from laughing.

"I need quiet," Dr. Broigen said coldly.

"We won't have any more screaming or fire-crackers, sir," I promised.

"Good," Dr. Broigen said and left.

We all looked at my father who was still nodding. Finally he looked up at me and shrugged.

"No more firecrackers," I repeated.

He nodded and went back to the house.

"That was weird," Georgie said.

I said, "Yeah. He's really weird."

"Which one?" Ivy asked.

"That Grover scared me," Georgie said, flopping down on the floor. "What were those things, anyway, caps? Or were they really firecrackers?"

"I don't know. Help me fan the smoke out of here, will you, before we all suffocate or the place catches on fire."

Ivy and Georgie fanned and I went in for a can of lilac spray. It smells awful, but not as bad as the sulphur from Grover's bombs.

"I hate to say this," I said when we could breathe again, "but if this is Centerin City's talent, then we've really had it."

"Hi! Is this the audition?"

A smallish kid with brown curly hair and glasses was standing in the garage door blinking at us.

"Yeah . . . You play bass?"

"Yup!"

"What's your name?" I asked.

"I never tell anyone my name. You can call me by my initials. J.D."

"J.D.," Georgie repeated and gave me a look that clearly said "We are meeting every weirdo in town!"

"Yup. J.D. Ettinger."

Ivy perked up. "Ettinger?" she asked quickly. "Does your father own Ettinger's?"

J.D. nodded and smiled. "Yup," he said proudly.

Ettinger's was the biggest music store in Centerin City. If J.D. turned out to be any good . . .

We watched him begin to open up his rhinestone-studded guitar case.

"Listen, J.D.," I began while he got ready, "we're interested in a funky blues sound. We don't want to do all rock like everybody else. That's why we want to get a horn, too. You like that idea?"

He shrugged. "Sure. I need to get experience playing with a group. It's important to my career."

His career?

"What school do you go to, J.D.?" Georgie asked.

"I just graduated sixth grade from Latham."

"Oh, then you'll be starting C.C. Junior next month, right?"

"Yup."

We smiled at each other. Our age. Just like us. I thought, this might be it!

"Well, you want to start?" I asked. Ivy and I sat down at our instruments and Georgie picked up his guitar. "What do you know?"

"Well, uh, what do *you* want to do?"

"We'll do whatever you want," I said, "only we have to keep it down a little because we have a crazy neighbor next door. Okay?"

"Okay. But you pick it."

"Well, look, J.D., it's your audition. What do you feel comfortable with?"

"I've been playing rock . . ."

"Well, okay . . . for now . . . but keep it down. What tune?"

"Um . . ."

"Just name something, anything," Georgie said impatiently.

"Uh . . ."

"Elton John? The Outlaws? Kiss? What?"

"Uh . . ."

I was sorry I'd told him to keep it quiet. Now he wasn't making a sound. And he sure looked awkward with that beautiful guitar. Was he shy? How come he couldn't think of even one tune?

We had fooled around a little with an Elton John tune that Georgie sang called *Benny and the Jets,* so we suggested that we mess a little with that and

J.D. could play changes and fill in. He said, "Okay," and we started to play, but he immediately screwed up.

"I don't know that real well," he said apologetically.

"Okay, then. There's a good bass solo in *Nobody Knows*," Ivy suggested. "You know that? Paul McCartney?"

"Mm-mm," he said, shaking his head.

"Well, what *do* you know?" I said finally.

"Why don't you just—you know—play a few licks, so we can hear you by yourself," Georgie suggested.

"Uh, okay," J.D. muttered. He fumbled around with a bassline.

"You can't play, can you?" Ivy said. She sounded so disappointed.

"I've only had three lessons," J.D. said sadly.

"Three lessons—Geez!"

"I really want to get in with a group so bad," he said. "Let me join. I'll learn as I go along. You won't even hear me in the beginning."

"We don't want a bass we can't even hear," Georgie said.

"We can't use you, J.D.," I said, shaking my head.

"Aw, please, come on, plee-eze?"

I looked sideways at Ivy.

"We can't, J.D. I'm really sorry. We need someone who can play."

"I'll learn. I will. Come on. Look, I'll tell you what. You let me join and I'll guarantee fabulous discounts for you at the store. Anything you want. I'll bet my father would even give you free stuff if you let me join."

We looked at each other.

Georgie said, "Well . . . maybe we could—"

But I interrupted. "We'll have to talk about it, J.D. And we have other people to hear. Look, I'll give you a call, okay?"

"Will you call me tonight? Huh? Huh?" he begged.

"Sure, sure. Tonight," I said. He packed up his gorgeous top-of-the-line bass in its beautiful gaudy case and left.

"Take him," Georgie said as soon as he was gone. "Take him, we'll teach him."

"Roto-toms," Ivy said.

"What?"

"Roto-toms. A set of three lists for almost three hundred dollars. I've always wanted a set of roto-toms."

"Ivy . . ."

"He's so enthusiastic. Don't you think he can learn while he works with us?"

"He tried to bribe us," I said. "He whines, like a little kid. He's probably so used to getting what he wants that he thinks he can join a band without knowing a note. Three lessons, come on!"

"Well, I don't see people breaking down the

doors to get in here, do you?" Georgie asked. "I could use some new strings . . . and look at my case. It's got a hole in it."

"Look, I could use a new amp, too, but I don't think we should compromise our standards. Besides, we don't even know if he's got any talent, or if he'd quit the minute the work was too hard or he got bored. I don't even like him. He's pushy."

Ivy made a face. "I didn't really like him much, either."

"I don't think it's right to bribe people," I said. "We're sitting here talking about him . . . we wouldn't even consider using him if he hadn't thrown in that stuff about the discounts."

"I know . . ."

We all looked at the floor for a while.

"So here we are . . . Nobody's beating down our door . . . We have no horn, unless we start a band that plays military drills . . . and we don't even have a bass. I thought that one'd be easy."

"I thought it'd all be easy," Georgie sighed.

That night I called J.D. Ettinger and told him to come around again when he learned how to play. He didn't take it well. I had to hold the phone away from my ear while he whined. I tried to be as nice as I could but when he saw I wasn't budging he got nasty.

"You'll be sorry," he said. "You're passing up a

good thing. When I got home I asked my father for horn lessons, too. And maybe banjo!"

Just what I thought. He didn't know or care anything about music, he just wanted what he wanted when he wanted it.

I interrupted him while he was carrying on about flugelhorn and clarinet.

"Look, J.D., if you can learn all those instruments, you won't need us at all. You'll be a one-man band!" I hung up.

The next day we met in my garage as usual. We all thought we'd be rehearsing with our new horn and new bass by then, but nobody said it.

"Why don't we practice?" I said, flexing my fingers.

Georgie said, "Aw . . ." and looked at the floor.

I looked at Ivy and she looked at me.

"This's really a bummer, y'know?" Georgie said. "Things always start out great and look how they end up. First we find each other and then our sound's no good. Then we have to find a new practice place . . . And then we find our sound and hold this great open audition and look who shows up! Boy, if we do get a bass and horn they'll probably come down with the mumps or something right after we get good!"

Ivy and I looked at each other again. Then she said, *"Mo-oan!"* And I said, *"Gro-oan!"* and Ivy said, *"Sob, sob, sob."*

Georgie grinned sheepishly. "Come on . . ."

"Georgie," Ivy said, smiling, "you always look at things on the down side. " 'Come on' yourself!"

"She's right," I said. "You think we got this far

just to give up and moan and groan? We're gonna find our horn and our bass and until we do we just keep practicing whenever we can. And we don't stop looking."

"Even if we don't find anybody by the time school starts," Ivy said, "we'll get someone then. Don't forget, a lot of kids are away in the summer, and besides, most of our flyers were just around the neighborhood."

"Yeah," I said. "We should try downtown."

"Maybe, but there'll be new kids in junior high," Ivy said. "We're bound to find people, either in band or in orchestra or something . . ."

Georgie still looked glum, but not hopeless. "You think so?" he asked.

"I'll call my cousin Audrey again," I said. "We have to keep listening to those sixties groups to get our sound, right? Like Ham said. I'll bet Audrey and Arthur have more records they could tape for us. And we can pool some of our money and buy more. Let's canvass the neighborhood for everybody we know who's over twenty-five. I bet we could get dozens of songs to listen to!"

"We could have gotten all the records we need from Ettinger's at discount . . ." Georgie teased, and then Ivy and I knew he'd be all right.

We listened to Eric Clapton till our ears fell off. We listened to the horns on Blood, Sweat and

Tears. We listened to the Rolling Stones, Cream, the Blues Project, Chicago, Traffic, and some older guys, Buddy Holly, Les Paul. We had never heard of a lot of the groups, but even though it was older folks' music, the more we listened to it, the more we liked it. This music definitely needed a comeback. It was time. Just get us the right players and we'd make some scene, all right, just watch!

I could hardly wait for school to start again.

I had two classes with Georgie—English and Science—but none with Ivy, although all three of us had the same lunch period. I had a study hall with J. D. Ettinger who sneered at me the first day and ignored me after that. I wondered if he had enough guts to be still taking guitar, but I didn't ask him.

The day that after-school clubs were posted on the bulletin board, we tacked up our own notice. This time it said:

THE CENTERIN CITY BLUES TRIO
(keyboard, drums, lead guitar)

Wants a Challenging Blues Sound
Using Bass and Horn

If you play trumpet or trombone or bass guitar, please contact:

Ivy Sunday, Home Room 4
Eddie Levy, Home Room 30 or
George Redding, Home Room 10.

❧

Right from the beginning, Shelby Powell was a Man of Mystery. It's hard to describe, but it seemed to me that Shelby was always lugging a heavy bag of stuff which he could never put down or open up to show you or let you help him carry. Not that he really had such a bag, it just *seemed* that he did. Maybe it was the way he talked, kind of distant and shy, and also quick. Because if he talked slow you might remember something he said and ask him about it later.

At least those were the feelings I had when I first met him. It was the day after we put up our second audition notice and he was waiting for me in my Home Room. He came up to me quickly— a tall skinny black kid with big glasses—and asked if I were Eddie Levy. When I said I was, then he pulled back a little, the way a turtle does, into his shell.

"Are you in this Home Room?" I asked, not knowing who was supposed to speak next.

"Uh, no, I'm in eighth grade . . . but I wanted to ask you about, uh, the notice. Did you put that notice up? About the blues band?"

"Yeah," I said, brightening. "Do you play a horn or a bass guitar?"

"I play the . . . uh . . . trumpet."

I had a funny impression of the guy, and I wasn't sure whether I should be glad he answered the notice or not. I thought of J.D. Ettinger and asked the kid how long he'd been playing.

"Five years," he said.

"Oh. You must be pretty good, huh?"

His face lit up with a slow smile. "Yeah," he said. "I'm good."

I smiled back. He felt confident about his music and that was okay.

"Well, what's your name?" I asked.

"Oh. Sorry. Shelby. Shelby Powell."

"Hi."

"Hi."

My turn again. "You play in the school band?" I asked.

"Oh, no," he said quickly. "I mean . . . I never played with a group, but I'd like to. A lot. I—I've always wanted to—"

"How come you didn't join the school band?"

"Uh, well, I didn't have the opportunity before, besides, a blues group sounds interesting, say maybe you could just let me play for you and then when you hear what I can do then you decide." He said it all in one breath. I forgot the question I asked him.

"Well, great," I said. "Want to come over to my house after school? We've been using my garage to practice in—"

"Can it be *right* after school?" he asked. "I

mean—I could be at your house by three . . . Uh, where do you live?"

I told him.

"Oh. Sure. No problem."

"Well, great," I said again, hoping it was.

"A horn! Oh, terrific!" Ivy cried when I told her, and she and Georgie called their parents to say they'd be home later than usual. We raced to my house and got there before Shelby.

Ivy kept an old snare drum and a set of traps in our garage for when we practiced. She kept her good drum set at home, but sometimes her brother, Raymond, who worked at their parents' grocery store, would shlep them over for her if she really wanted them for something special. To pay him back, she'd sometimes take over for him in the store.

"Should I call Raymond?" Ivy asked while we were waiting for Shelby. Maybe I should have the whole set here to show him how we sound."

"I don't think you need it," I told her. "We'll be listening to *him,* mostly, and if he works out, then maybe tomorrow we can have the drums here—"

"Hi, is this the place?"

It was exactly three o'clock and Shelby, hugging a gorgeous leather trumpet case, was smiling from the doorway and panting as though he'd run all the way.

"This is the place, open your case," I said, and

when he took out that gleaming metal instrument, he handled it so lovingly I had to shake my head.

Well, he played his horn. I didn't know what it was he played and I sure didn't care, it was just so great to listen to him. Ivy was absolutely goggle-eyed and Georgie just kept nodding his head up and down and grinning.

"Hey, Shelby?" I said when he was through. "What was that, anyway?"

"I wrote it myself," he said and kind of ducked his head.

"Wow!" Ivy said.

"You're hired!" Georgie screamed and when Ivy and I glared at him, he looked sheepish. "I'm sorry," he said. "I guess we should consult each other."

"Right," I said.

"Right," Ivy said.

"Okay, let's consult," Georgie said. "Okay with you?"

"Uh huh."

"Okay with you?"

"Yep."

"You're hired!" Georgie cried and this time we all yelled with him!

Shelby looked as if he'd just won the Academy Award. "I really appreciate this, I really do," he babbled. "I can't wait to start, I mean, this is just great, really—"

"But wait, Shelby," I began. "You know, you

haven't heard us even play a note yet. When can we all get together?"

"I'm really going to be in a blues band! I can't believe it!" Shelby said, shaking his head. "A blues— Oh. When can we get together? Is that what you said?" His face suddenly rearranged itself.

"Yeah, that's what I said, Shel. When can we get together?"

"Oh. Oh. Right. Um . . . any day but Wednesday is fine. And right after school. See, I have to be home by five. Is that possible? Is that okay?"

"It's okay with me," Ivy said, looking right at Shelby and smiling. "Oh, except one day I have to help in the store . . ."

"I have guitar lessons on Thursday," Georgie said. "Gee, that leaves us only three days. Unless you can work on weekends . . ."

"No!" Shelby blurted. "I mean . . . no, weekends are out . . ."

"But that's when we'll be playing jobs!"

"Oh, well, I mean, the evenings . . . the nights should be all right." He frowned and looked at the floor. "Sure, the jobs'd be okay, but it'll be hard for me to . . . practice during the day."

"Well," I finally said, "there's more of a problem. *My* piano lessons are on Tuesdays, which would leave us only *two* rehearsal days."

"Oh, boy . . ." Georgie sighed.

"No, wait a minute, tell you what," I said. "If

you can change your guitar lesson to Wednesday, Georgie, I'll try to switch mine, too, so we can get all four other days to practice."

"And I'll help in the store on Wednesdays, too!" Ivy said.

"Okay . . . we all have our lessons and work days on Wednesday," Georgie said, chewing it over. "That'll be good if we can work it."

"Fine!" Shelby said almost formally, and beamed.

We gave him four of our tapes to take home and listen to.

I was kind of glad that Georgie left at the same time Shelby did because I wanted to talk to Ivy. I had this funny feeling about Shelby and I wanted to see if she did, too.

So I asked, "What do you think?"

"About what?"

"Shelby Powell, of course!"

"He's fantastic," she said calmly, picking up her book bag.

"Oh . . . yeah, he can play, all right, I didn't mean that. I mean, do you get funny vibes from him. As a person. Isn't he a little mysterious to you?"

"Huh?"

"Listen, Ivy, I can't put my finger on it!" I said impatiently. "It's just that he seems like he's hiding stuff, or he doesn't want to talk about himself or something. I don't know, just *something!* Don't you get that?"

"No. I think he's shy. And real nice. And he can really play, Eddie."

"Oh, I know that . . . And it's not that I don't like him, either. It's only that I'm used to being up front and when I don't think someone else is, then it makes me feel kind of funny, that's all."

Ivy just looked at me. I guessed this was one time we weren't on the same wave length.

"Well, I really am glad we've got him in the band, though," I said.

"Me, too," from Ivy.

❁

"Ma, if Ham can take me on Wednesdays, is that okay with you?"

"What's wrong with Tuesdays?"

I told her.

"Listen, Eddie, my little musician genius, while you're organizing your life so well, you have to remember you're organizing mine, too. Tuesday is the day I wanted so that when I'm driving your sister to her ballet class I can drive you to your piano lesson right after, then go back and pick up your sister on the way home and do it all in one trip on one day, do you see?"

"Yeah, but—"

"Sh. Wednesday is my afternoon to help your father with his envelope-stuffing-and-whatnot."

"Yeah, but—"

"Sh. If Yvonne can't switch her class to Wednesday, then I'll have Tuesday her and Wednesday you and my week will be *farblunget*."

"Yeah, but—"

"Sh. And what about Hebrew school, Eddie? You haven't even taken that into account. Now you can speak."

"Okay. I have thought about Hebrew school." This was my bar mitzvah year and I had to go three times a week to Hebrew: once for chanting and bar mitzvah class and twice for Hebrew culture and stuff. "It'll still be okay because the two classes during the week are at five-thirty and I can still walk and be there on time. The Sunday class is no problem."

My mother frowned.

"Look," I said. "How about if you drive me on Wednesdays, then maybe Pop can bring home the work you help him with and I can do it at night, after I finish my homework."

She smiled and touched my face. "That's some schedule, Eddie, my little musician genius." Then she sighed. "We'll work it out," she said.

Terrific! Now all I had to do was get Ham to say Wednesdays were okay.

They were, so that part was fine. There might have been a snag because Georgie couldn't switch his lesson day from Thursday to Wednesday, but he did manage to get himself a five-thirty spot and since the Mystery Man had to be home by five anyway and I had Hebrew at five-thirty, we still got in four good days.

The first day we got together, Shelby was funny. He said, "Where's the music?"

"We don't use it most of the time. We improvise. We want a sound like on those tapes we gave you."

"Oh."

"Did you listen to them, Shel?"

"Some."

"How much is 'some'?"

"Two cuts. I'm sorry . . . It's the time . . . I don't have much . . ." He trailed off. "I'll do okay, it's just that I'm used to having the music right there in front of me all the time."

"The thing you played for us that you made up—that was improvising, wasn't it?"

"Oh, no! That was a composition. I wrote it down and memorized it."

Ivy said, "Wow" again. She said it a lot around Shelby.

"Don't panic," Shelby said, holding up his hand. "I can do it. Maybe I haven't improvised very much, but I can do it. Now, look, you know *Spinning Wheel?*"

"Sure, it was on one of the tapes we gave you."

"Well, it was one of the cuts I listened to. There's a good trumpet solo on it and maybe I can improvise one of my own. Shall we try it?"

Sometimes he sounded so formal. Nice, but formal.

"Well, okay. Ready? One . . . two . . . one, two, three, four—"

We played. Shelby did the right "blats" on beats two and four and then he came in with a trumpet solo. It wasn't like on the record, though. It was weird. And long. And he went right over the beginning of the next phrase.

We stopped.

"Hey, I'm sorry, I know what I did. It won't happen again, it was too long."

"Well, yeah, it was, but it was good. Weird, but good. What was that, anyway?"

"It was just a little bit of, uh, *Jesu, Joy of Man's Desiring.*"

"It was what?"

"*Jesu, Joy of Man's Desiring.* I meant to do just a little riff but I got carried away."

"A little *riff* of *Jesu, Joy of Man's Desiring?*" Ivy gurgled. And then she said, "Wow!"

"I thought a classical riff would fit in. Sound nice."

"It did, it did," I said. "But cut it down."

It worked.

"How much did you play that cut of *Spinning Wheel?*" I asked Shelby when we were through.

"Once," he said.

I nodded. It figured. Shelby was a musician.

The rehearsals were a blast! We still didn't have a bass, which was probably hardest on me, but we went to work in earnest, and since we all cared so much and played well, it was the most fun I'd ever had. I told Ham all about it, naturally.

"Ah, sounds good, Eddie."

"Oh, it's fun, all right, I love what we're playing. But my left hand's about to go on strike."

"Yeah, I know, but without a bass, buddy, that hand's got to work overtime. Wish I could help you, but I don't know anyone in Centerin City. You put up your notice anywhere else besides school?"

"Not since the summer."

"Well, why don't you try getting them around town. Can't hurt."

"Right."

WANTED: BASS GUITAR PLAYER FOR BLUES BAND
MUST BE FOURTEEN OR UNDER
CALL EDDIE: 555-4234

We followed Ham's advice and tacked up our notices on telephone poles around town as well as

73

on the school bulletin board, and the first night I got a call:

"Is this Eddie who wants a bass player?"

"Yes . . ."

"BLAAAGGGHHHH!" the voice said and the phone was slammed down in my ear.

I was sure it was J.D. Ettinger.

"Eddie."

"Yes, Pop?"

"Your music is going well? You've added a horn now?"

"A trumpet. Shelby Powell. You'll meet him soon, Pop, he's really good, but he can never stay past about quarter-to-five."

"Your mother says it sounds loud in there. In the garage."

"She doesn't like it?"

"No, no, you know your mother, she loves that you're making music. I was thinking about Dr. Broigen."

"No problem! Shelby's been with us a couple of weeks now and we haven't heard a word from Broigen. Him and his chestnut trees. What is he, anyway?"

"He's a plant pathologist."

"Oh."

"Haven't you been wondering why you haven't heard him complain lately?"

"No . . ."

"Well, I'll tell you the reason. It's because he's

not home. Your sister's been watering his plants and feeding his cats."

"She has?"

"You've been very busy, Eddie, you haven't noticed. Dr. Broigen is in Michigan."

"What's he doing there?"

"There are eight groves of trees in Michigan that have survived the blight. He's out there studying them."

"Oh. Great!"

"Not great. He's coming back soon and now that you're adding musicians to your group you might be in for some trouble. From him. You'd better think about that."

"But Pop, we only practice in the afternoons after school. It's not as if we play loud at night or anything . . ."

"I'm just telling you."

"Yeah, okay, Pop, thanks."

I couldn't worry about Mr. Broigen and his chestnut trees. I had much more important things to think about like where we were going to get our bass. Every night I sat by the phone, but nothing happened.

As it turned out, our bass player didn't phone. He kind of hunched up to me on my way out of school one afternoon in late October. Just as we had begun to think there were no bass players anywhere near Centerin City!

"You Eddie?"

"Yeah . . ."

"I wanna talk to you."

"I'm in a hurry," I said. I was. We had to get to practice before Shelby the Mystery Man had to go home.

"You want a bass player or not?"

I stopped and looked him over. He was kind of mangy-looking and he had his hair all slicked back except for one curl that hung down over his forehead.

"You mean you?" I asked stupidly.

"Yeah, me, what's wrong with that?"

"Nothing. Nothing. You have to audition, though."

"Yeah, okay. When, now?"

"Now is fine. We're rehearsing at my house. Out in back, in the garage. Where's your axe?"

"I'll get it. Where do you live?"

"24 Coral."

"I'll be there."

"You have to be there soon. We quit at four-forty-five."

"You punch a clock?"

"It's a long story. What's your name?"

"Reese."

"First or last?"

"Both."

I barely had enough time to explain about Reese to the others before he showed up. He was carrying a burlap bag and the smallest amp I'd ever seen.

I introduced him to Ivy and Shelby and Georgie, whose eyebrows went through his hairline as Reese pulled his guitar out of the bag.

"Where do I plug in?" Reese asked, holding the power cord from his amp and looking around.

"You're not going to get any power out of that thing," Georgie wailed. "When was it made, 1909? That's no bass amp, that toy'll never give you any bottom!"

"Oh, yeah?" Reese snarled.

Things were getting off to a flying start. I elbowed Georgie who decided that amends were in order.

"Hey. I'm sorry. Look, the outlet's over there, but why don't you plug into my amp, okay?" And then he added, "I didn't mean anything . . ."

Reese accepted the apology by plugging into Georgie's amp.

"What'll you have?" I asked Reese.

*"Crossroads,"* he answered, and then it was my turn for raised eyebrows.

"Really?" I asked.

"You're a blues band, aren't you? That's what the sign said."

"Yeah, we sure are!" I cried. *"Crossroads* is a great number! Shelby does a terrific wah-wah trumpet in that, don't you, Shel? Hey, you like Eric Clapton?"

"My brother says Eric Clapton is the best guitarist in the world."

"What's your brother play?" Ivy asked.

"Bass. Same as me. He taught me."

"How come he didn't come around to audition?"

Reese laughed.

"What's so funny?"

"Nothin', man. He's twenty-eight years old, anyway, he got no time for band-playin'."

"All right," I said, sitting down at my keyboard, "let's do it, one . . . two . . . one, two, three, four—"

When the song was over, we chewed our lips and nodded our heads at each other.

"He sure was right on top of the beat," Ivy said.

"Whatever changes I played, he heard," I added.

"Good beat," Georgie said. "Very nice."

Shelby smiled. "He seems real good," he said.

"You got a job with us if you want it, Reese," I said.

"You guys make any money?" he asked.

"Not yet. We just completed our band. Now we have to go to work, build up a repertoire, learn to work together. Then we can advertise and stuff."

Ivy said, "If we try real hard, maybe we can be ready by Christmas and pick up on all the holiday parties!"

"Yeah! Well, let's start right now! How about it?" I cried. "Let's do *Crossroads* again, let's see what we can do this time."

We were halfway through it when the garage door burst open.

We stopped instantly. Ivy muttered, "Uh oh."

"Welcome home, Mr. Broigen," I sighed.

"*Doctor* Broigen. And this is not what I consider a welcome. I thought you said this wasn't going to continue, Eddie."

I wanted to say "It's Edward," but I didn't. I said, "Well, I promised there wouldn't be any more firecrackers, Dr. Broigen, and there won't be."

"I can't work with this, Eddie. You're going to have to find another place to practice. Besides, it's getting cold now. Aren't you cold working in here?"

"No . . . we're not cold . . ."

"Who's *that,* man?" Reese asked, jerking his head toward Broigen.

"Our neighbor. Dr. Broigen. He works at his house right next door."

"What's your problem, man?" Reese asked, looking directly at him. "What is it, music bother you or something?"

Dr. Broigen opened his mouth but nothing came out. His face was purple.

"Listen, stay cool," Reese said, as Ivy covered her mouth to stifle a giggle. "We're not here to inter-fere with anyone's work, right?" Reese looked at the four of us but didn't wait for our answer. "Right," he said, "so don't worry about it, man. I'll take care of it."

Mr.—*Dr.* Broigen looked at me. I looked at Reese and shrugged. "He'll take care of it," I said and prayed silently.

"What're you starin' at *me* for?" Reese asked after Dr. Broigen left.

"This is our only practice place," I said. "How are you going to take care of the sound? What can you do?"

Reese put up both his palms and closed his eyes. "I said I'd take care of it and I'll take care of it. You got the word of Reese."

I decided to take the word of Reese. I still didn't want to worry about Broigen. Now, just when our band was complete I only wanted to think about that. I told Reese when we rehearsed and he said it was okay with him. He wouldn't tell us what grade he was in or even how old he was. He seemed mysterious, too, although not in the way Shelby was.

"It doesn't matter," Ivy said, as I walked her home that afternoon. "If he shows up and works hard and we have a good group with a new sound, that's what matters."

"But don't you wonder, though? Don't you wonder why shy ol' Shelby gets hyper if a tune runs over four-forty-five? Don't you wonder about Reese and why he won't even say what grade he's in?"

"Yeah, I wonder," she said, "but I don't lose sleep over it. Neither should you."

"Oh, I don't, I don't. But . . . remember when we were talking about special friends and being up front and all that?"

"Uh huh . . ."

"Well, you're like that with me . . . and so is Ham, I guess, but Ham's pretty laid back most of the time . . ."

"But Shelby's not that kind of special friend? Is that what you mean? Because he doesn't talk about himself much, or Reese either?"

"Maybe," I answered. "But not exactly. I mean, Georgie's pretty straight and I like him, it's just more than that. I tried to tell you before . . . You know, before we started working together last year—before all our free time was taken up practicing and stuff—I had a couple of friends, guys I used to hang out with—used to play D and D with them all the time . . ."

"Me, too," she said. "I mean, I had some girl-friends I just don't see any more."

"Yeah, same with me. But you know, I don't really mind it so much because I always have somebody to talk to about anything. You. I guess you're my best friend, Ivy." I wasn't sure if she knew, so I thought I'd better tell her.

"Does that bother you?" she asked after a minute. It wasn't the response I had expected.

"Bother me? No! What do you mean, *bother* me?"

"Well, for one thing, I'm a girl."

"No kidding."

"Usually twelve-year-old boys don't have best friends who are girls. Not to mention that I'm black and Presbyterian and you're white and Jewish, and—"

"Hey, Ivy, does it bother *you?*" I interrupted.

"Not at all," she said firmly. "You're my best friend now, too. Only sometimes I think about what other people think."

"What difference does that—"

"Not that what other people think is going to change me, no way," she said. "What I want is to play drums and be in a blues band and have you for my best friend and I want all that to go on forever and ever. The thing is, though, I know that makes me different from other girls my age and sometimes I wonder about that and when you said just now that I was your best friend I knew you were wondering about it too. That's all."

"Oh. Well, yeah, I know what you mean. But our music for example— We want that to be different . . . to stand out from other groups, right?"

"Oh, sure, but there's 'different' and 'different'," she said. "You can stand out by wearing freaky clothes, too, y'know . . ." She laughed.

"Listen," I said, "even if stupid people think we're all freaks right now, I don't even care. We'll show them when we start working. I've never seen such talented people as us, have you?"

"No, you're right," she said. "There never have been such talented people as we are."

❄

The next afternoon when Ivy, Georgie, Shelby, and I arrived at the garage after school, Reese was standing in front of it, leaning against the door. My mother was standing next to him, smiling. Now what was this?

"Ma?"

"We have a surprise for you," she said.

"We?"

"Your friend Reese and I." She winked conspiratorially at Reese who winked back. Talk about your odd couple!

"Well, . . . let's not keep them in suspense," my mother said and flung open the garage door.

The four of us stood there gawking. The walls of the garage were covered with—mattresses.

"Ma?" I said. Ivy's jaw was hanging down.

"Instant soundproofing!" my mother cried.

"And insulation!" Reese added. "Energy-saving, like the government wants." He folded his arms across his chest.

"Wha— Where did they come from?"

My mother spread her hands. "Listen," she said, this morning, right after you left for school, there I was, scouring out the bathroom sink, when my eye catches on something crawling down the

84

driveway toward the garage. I put down the Brillo and go over to the window and I see what it is crawling. A mattress."

"Huh?"

"It's a mattress, only it isn't crawling by itself. Reese is under it. I go out there and stand in front of him as he's about to drop it on the ground here. 'Why are you dropping a mattress in front of my garage?' I say. 'And why aren't you in school, you're just a kid.' "

Reese opened his mouth then, but my mother said, "Sh! So the second question he doesn't answer but the first he says, 'It isn't just one mattress I'm delivering, it's twelve.' I say, '*Twelve mattresses?* I didn't even order one!' "

Reese and I both opened our mouths then, but my mother said, "Sh! So he explains how he got this idea to soundproof the garage so Dr. Broigen can cure his chestnut tree blight in peace and you musicians can go on with your work uninterrupted. And he said how it would keep out the draft and wind. He said if he worked all day he could probably get five mattresses over here before you got home from school."

"Hey, Reese," I said, beginning to recover a little. "That was a great idea!"

"Yeah, but you got more than five here," Georgie said.

Reese turned to me. "Your mother," he said, "she got her car and helped. We piled the mattresses on the roof and both of us put 'em up on the walls."

I looked around and shook my head. The mattresses sure didn't look like the kind you'd find on the beds at the Ritz Hotel. They were dirty and stained and had stuffing popping out of them all over the place. Not that I cared about that because they sure would solve our problems, but I was curious.

"Where'd you get them, Reese?" I asked. "Twelve mattresses."

"From buildings," Reese answered with a shrug.

"He had them piled up on the street when I met him with the car," my mother said. "We made two trips."

"Buildings?" Ivy repeated. Shelby and Georgie went inside to inspect the nailing-up job.

"Yeah, you know, abandoned buildings. There's plenty of junk in those places—you'd be surprised. You could live for a long time in one of those. People do, y'know."

"Is that where you live?" I asked. "In one of those?"

Reese stiffened. "No! A-course not. But I know 'em. I used to play there when I was a kid. There's lots of things I know."

"*No*body has said 'thank you'," my mother said harshly.

I grinned. "Thank you," I said. "Thanks, Ma! Thanks, Reese! That's really terrific, really."

"It's great, Reese," Ivy said. "Thanks."

Shelby said, "Thanks, both of you," and Georgie cried, "Now we're really all set!"

Look, I'm not bragging. I don't brag. But we really *were* good. Somehow we lucked out in getting together and in all of us digging the same music. And even if two of us were a little mysterious, it didn't affect the way we played or got along . . . most of the time.

GEORGIE: Let's do this in E.

ME: E's too brittle, do it in E♭.

GEORGIE: Yeah, but my voice squeaks on that top F.

IVY: Sing it in falsetto, then!

ME: Ivy, that's too loud. How about using brushes there instead of sticks? I can't even hear my own solo.

IVY: Loud: I'm never loud! Whaddya mean *loud?*

GEORGIE: Hey, Reese, I know you want to kick us along, but are you trying to set a record for the number of notes you can get into every measure?

REESE: In your ear, Carrothead!

REESE: Shelby, that sounds like 'elevator music'! Can't you get a little *bite* in that horn?

SHELBY: Bite? Reese, did you ever hear the word 'subtle'?

Okay, nobody's perfect. Sure, we argued, but it was always about the music and all five of us really cared about how each song came across. We were five people all working toward making the Centerin City Blues Band something that people would enjoy and remember. And just keeping that in mind was what made us argue and what made us happy.

I guess I'd better mention that we changed our name shortly after Reese joined up. First, we were a trio and then when we expanded we were a band. We knew we'd need some kind of new catchy handle and we mumbled about it every now and then but mostly we were too busy practicing to give it much thought. That is, until Reese's guitar fell apart.

## 7.

We'd started teasing him about that guitar.

"I know where you got that axe, Reese," Georgie'd say. "It was the prize in a Cracker Jacks box, right?"

And Reese would get sore and growl, "Yeah, you wanna see how it tastes, Redding?"

But after a while, Reese would kid about it, too. He called it his "CARE package," and he found a little Fresh Air Fund sticker that he slapped on the back of it that read "Send a child to camp." It was a piece of junk and he knew it and one day the seams just split on him in the middle of a riff and a string twanged and it was dead. The closest I'd seen Reese come to getting emotional was when that old friend of his died.

"It was my brother's guitar," he said, his voice cracking.

"We could bury it," Georgie suggested, "and give it a nice funeral, Reese."

"Shut up!" Reese cried and Georgie knew this wasn't the time for kidding. We all just sat there, looking at the guitar and then at the floor.

It was funny about Reese. We never saw him in

school. Even though he came on pretty wise and tough, I was pretty sure he wasn't much over thirteen. Maybe fourteen, tops, but I doubted it. And he never had any books from school at practice, never talked about homework or exams like the rest of us, never even put down any teachers. In fact, the only personal thing he ever did talk about was his brother and even then, he didn't say much. Sometimes he talked about visiting him—on Sundays—and sometimes he talked about his brother's music, but it was still pretty sketchy. I kind of had an idea about Reese's brother, but I never said anything about it, even to Ivy.

Well, when the guitar died, Reese seemed to crack a little bit.

"I was supposed to take care of it while he was gone . . ." he said. He was almost whispering.

Well, geez, Reese, you couldn't help it," Georgie said comfortingly. "Look at the thing, I mean it was held together with just love and appreciation and Scotch tape, for Pete's sake . . ."

"I know how you feel though," Shelby said, shaking his head. "It was your friend."

"More'n that," Reese mumbled.

I decided we should get onto practical matters and that would break the gloom.

"Okay," I said, finally. "The king is dead, what do we use for the heir-to-the-throne?"

Reese said, "Huh?"

"What are you going to play now?" I asked.

"You're a bass player without a bass. You don't have the money for a new one, do you?"

Reese barked.

"That's what I figured."

"Maybe we better let J.D. Ettinger join the band," Georgie suggested and I whacked him lightly with what was left of Reese's guitar as he yelled, "Think of the discounts!"

"Now, come on," I said, "let's think constructively. Somewhere there's a bass guitar with Reese's name on it."

"I'll get one," Reese said quietly.

"Where?" I asked.

"Never mind."

"Hey, Reese," I said as nicely as I could. "Where's your brother?" Maybe I should have waited until I got him alone to ask, but something inside me said that this was something we should all share if we could—so Reese would know he had friends. He said what I figured he would.

"None-a your damn business."

"It's okay, Reese," I said. "You can tell us. We really want to help."

"Ah, you probably know, right? He's in jail."

"What for?" Georgie asked.

Reese started to laugh. He laughed until tears leaked out of his eyes. We started to laugh a little, too, but kind of hesitatingly.

"Come on, Reese, what's he in the slammer for?" Georgie prodded.

"Aw, leave him alone," Ivy said. "You don't have to tell, Reese, if you don't want to—"

"Naw, naw . . . the reason I'm laughing . . . See, he's in for petty theft."

"What's funny about that?" Shelby asked.

"He was caught lifting a guitar! They caught him swiping an axe! For me! See, he wanted one for me, so we would each have one and he could teach me and all. That's the funny thing. I mean, it's so stupid. He goes to jail for trying to get me a guitar and I end up with *his* guitar which breaks anyway. Ahhh, it's so stupid!"

"What about your mother and father?" Ivy asked.

"Never met 'em," Reese answered.

"Where do you live, then?" I asked.

"Look, let's not get into my whole life story, okay? I told you about my brother because he had this idea last Sunday."

"What idea?"

"He thought he could do the arrangements. For our band. He's really good, I'm not puttin' you on."

"Aw, how can your brother—What's his name, anyway?"

"Reese!" Reese snorted.

"Right. Figures," I said. "Okay, how can Reese—your brother—do arrangements for us when he's in jail? He can't even hear us."

"He doesn't have to. He hears it in his head. I told him what we've got and he can hear it all.

92

And see, this stuff, this is his music. This is what he's always played, he grew up with it. He can do some dynamite arrangements for us, believe me!"

"How would we get 'em?" I asked.

"We figured that out last week, too. Tapes. Cassette tapes. He'd record all his ideas and I'd bring the tapes back on Sunday night, after visiting day. Then we could record for him and give him more ideas."

I waved my hand.

"How about just giving it a try, huh, Eddie?" It was the first time I'd ever heard Reese call me by name like that. It was nice.

"Sure, Reese, I'd be willing to try, but meanwhile, you don't have an instrument. And you're not going to be stupid enough to get one like your brother did."

"Yeah," he growled and sat down on a stool.

"Do we have any money left over from the summer?" I asked the group.

"No," Ivy said. "I had to spend mine for school clothes and supplies. Besides, there wasn't that much."

"My mother puts any money I make in the bank," Georgie said. "And she holds the bank book. So much for *my* money."

"I don't have any left either," I said.

"I went to music camp," Shelby said. "I didn't even earn any money."

"I could steal it," Reese said, but we ignored him.

"We can't ask our parents," I said.

"No way!"

"Forget it!"

"I can't, I can't," Shelby said. He looked so sad. "But—" he brightened. "I have something—"

"An idea?"

"Better than that."

"*What?*"

"Do you know anything about coins?" he asked.

"*Coins?*"

"Coins, yeah," Shelby said.

Reese said, "Yeah, they put them in your eyes when you die if you happen to be an ancient Greek!"

"How do you know that?" I asked.

"I know a lot of stuff," he snapped. "Anyway, I also know that coins go in slot machines. That I probably know better than anybody!"

"Slot machines, right," Shelby said, grinning. "You know those penny arcades they have at the beach? On the boardwalk? All those games?"

"Are you kidding?" Reese laughed. "That's where I spend my summer vacations!"

"Well," Shelby continued, "I only spent one day there, and it was two years ago. But I know something about coins and because of that, it was a very profitable day for me. Out there at the beach."

"Speak, Shelby!" I yelled, getting impatient.

"I have a coin collection. My parents started one for me when I was little. It's not a big deal, but it started me looking at any coins that came my way.

Just looking, y'know? Special dates, pictures, condition . . ."

"*So?*"

"So I got some change for the games that day and I automatically checked the coins the guy handed me. I always do that. One of the coins was a 1937 buffalo nickel."

"Is that good?"

"Well, it can be. And this one was. See the right foreleg on the buffalo was missing."

"That makes it valuable, right?" Ivy cried. "If there's something wrong with the way they print it, that makes it worth more money!"

"The way they *mint* it, Ivy. And that's right. This 37 D buffalo nickel is worth a lot more than a nickel."

"Shelby, hey—"

"My parents don't know about it. It was one thing I kept to myself. I always thought . . . someday it would come in handy. For an emergency. This is an emergency, right?"

"Wait a minute, Shel—" I said.

"No, Eddie, I really want to do this. How much can you get a good guitar for, Reese?"

"Ain't no nickel gonna buy what I saw yesterday."

"How much, Reese?"

"Saw a nice bass in a pawn shop downtown. It's a good one, the guy let me see it. He wants two hundred."

Shelby nodded.

"See, Shelby? How much is that five-cent piece of yours worth?"

"Six hundred dollars," Shelby said calmly.

Nobody spoke.

Then Georgie said, "You're kidding."

"Nope."

*"You got a six hundred dollar nickel?"* Reese screamed.

"Yep."

*"Where?"*

"In my piggy bank."

❖

There was a little store downtown that sold jewelry and antiques and things and it had a little sign out front: "We buy coins, gold, silver."

I'd never paid any attention to that store before but Shelby'd been in there a few times to talk to the owner about coins. It was the owner who'd told Shelby the real value of what he'd turned up on the boardwalk. And that when Shelby was ready to sell, he'd be ready to buy. You can make some good money with coins if you know what you're doing, and as Shelby pointed out, if you deal with reputable people.

The next morning, we met Shelby outside school. He'd brought his coin. It was in a tiny plastic envelope that you could see through.

"Don't touch it, don't squeeze it," Shelby cautioned. "Just look."

"Why?"

"Because you want it to be in the best condition. If it's handled too much it loses value."

"Getcher hands off it then!" Reese shrieked, jerking his hands away as if the coin were burning.

Shelby laughed. "It's all right, just don't grab at it, that's all. Let it rest on your palm. That's it . . ."

"Let's all go to the store this afternoon," Ivy said, jumping up and down. "For the sale."

"No, I'm not goin'," Reese said. "I don't want to jinx it."

"I couldn't stand the suspense," Georgie said. "I'd have a heart attack. What if the coin wasn't worth anything? What if you're wrong, Shelby?"

"I'm *not*, Georgie. The man saw it when I first found it. And I *know* him, it's not like I'm just a nobody off the street."

Georgie peered at the coin. "It's still only a nickel," he moaned. "How can that ol' nickel be worth so much money?"

"Okay, here's what we'll do," Ivy said. "Eddie, you go in with Shelby. I'll stay outside and play Florence Nightingale to these two worry birds until you're through." She turned to Shelby. "Shelby, this is real nice, what you're doing, and even if you don't get anything for your nickel, everyone will appreciate it, *won't they, Georgie and Reese?*" She flashed a withering look at the two of them.

"Sure," Georgie said and smiled sheepishly.

"Yeah, sure," Reese said. "I do, really, Shel."

Ivy said, "That's a good boy," and giggled.

"Don't worry about it," Shelby said. "It'll be okay. And I'm glad to do it. Really. We want our band to be the best!"

"We'll meet here right after school," I said.

"Yeah," Reese said with a grin. "Right after school. What time is that, anyway?"

❖

"Hey, Shelby Powell! How are ya, little buddy?"

"Hi, Frank. This's my friend, Eddie Levy."

"Eddie!"

"Hi."

"Frank?" Shelby said, pulling the little envelope out of his pocket and getting right to the point. "Remember that buffalo nickel I showed you?"

Frank frowned. "When was that, Shelby?"

My heart flipped over and I mentally shook myself. Now don't *you* start worrying like Georgie, I thought.

"Oh, a year, maybe a year-and-a-half ago," Shelby said.

Frank said, "Hmmmmm . . ."

"1937 D. Leg missing on the buffalo."

"Right foreleg?"

"Yup!"

"Sure do. That it?" Frank nodded toward the envelope in Shelby's hand.

Shelby put it on the table and Frank picked it up. Both of them had forgotten I was there so I was free to just gape. Frank was looking and looking at the coin, Shelby was looking and looking at Frank. I glanced out the front window but I couldn't see Ivy and the guys. I smiled to myself. Maybe she took them out for ice cream cones . . .

Frank clicked his tongue and said, "Shelby?"

"Yes?"

"You know, this is nicer than I remembered."

"It *is?*"

"Yah. Now look: all the detail of the buffalo is here—the horns, tail— See?"

"Uh huh, uh huh . . ."

"There are no nicks . . . Nope, no nicks. And it hasn't been cleaned, hasn't been played with . . ."

"How much, Frank?" Shelby whispered. I could see now he was as nervous as Reese and Georgie . . . and me.

"Ah, you ready to sell it?"

Shelby nodded hard.

"It's a very good coin, Shelby. Very good. I'll give you six hundred fifty."

The next sound was me, gasping for air.

"No kidding, six fifty?" Shelby asked.

"It's a fair price, Shelby," Frank said. "But I'll tell you what. Why don't I give you a receipt for the coin and you go and talk it over with your folks. Take a week. If there's any problem, you can have it back. I won't sell it till I hear from—"

"No, Frank. I don't need any receipt. Six hundred fifty is just fine."

They solemnly shook hands, while I just shook.

Shelby bought Reese the guitar he saw in the pawn shop and also a brand new amp; in return for that, Shelby gained Reese's undying devotion, which I'm not completely sure he needed.

Reese was forever polishing Shelby's horn, even while he was playing it, practically! He was always under Shelby's feet, trying to find ways to please him. Reese did everything but carry Shelby home.

"Reese, you gotta knock this off," Shelby said one day, after Reese had whipped Shelby's glasses off his face to wipe them.

"You know I'm going to pay it all back to you, Shelby," Reese said by way of acknowledgment. "I swear—you got a Bible, Eddie?"

"Aw, Reese . . ."

"No, Eddie, go get a Bible. Come on, I'm serious. I want witnesses to this."

I went into the house and got my father's Old Testament. Reese put his left hand on it and raised his right hand in the air.

"I swear before all these witnesses that as soon as this band makes money I'm going to give everything I earn to Shelby Powell until every nickel is paid back!" he intoned loudly. Then he burst out laughing, quickly lifting his hand from the Bible in case laughing would offend it.

"You hear that? 'Every *nickel*'? Well, I can't get that nickel back to you, Shel—"

"Come on, Reese, you're embarrassing me," Shelby said.

But Reese's face was now solemn. "You know,

100

in my whole life nobody ever even bought me a catcher's mitt or a bike or a new suit or anything. And here's ol' Shelby, a perfect stranger—"

"He's not a stranger," Ivy said. "He's a friend."

"I just won't forget it, that's all," Reese insisted.

"Me neither," I said. "It was some terrific thing to do."

Georgie said, "It sure was. *I'd* never have done it—"

"Well, we all benefited, didn't we?" Shelby said. "Reese got his axe and we got a band again."

"Then we have to re-name the band for Shelby," Reese announced.

I said, "Huh?"

"It's because of Shelby we've got our band. Let's call it the Shelby Powell Quintet!"

Shelby said, "No way!"

"Don't be modest, Shelby, you deserve it," Reese said, clapping him on the back.

"No, Reese, now let it go," Shelby said a little insistently.

"Look, how about this," Ivy said. "The Buffalo Nickel Blues Band."

I tried it out. "The Buff-a-lo Nick-el BluesBand. Hey, that has a nice ring to it!"

"Yeah, it does," Georgie said.

"The Buffalo Nickel Blues Band! Yeah, I like it! Is *that* okay with you, Shel?"

Shelby said formally, "I am honored." And he bowed.

It was very interesting receiving our arrangements from the Centerin City Jail where Reese's brother was doing his time. Getting arrangements *at all* was interesting, because before that what we did was improvise and—well, I guess we copied the records, mostly.

What we got from jail was what we began to call "talking music," although he actually ended up humming or singing all the parts by the end of each tape.

For example, for this tune called *God Bless the Child,* he sent back a tape that went:

"I hear the horn part in my head, it goes something like this—da-da-da—da-da da-a-a-a- and you put that in between the verses, and then between the phrases you could do a two-or-three note fill— not too much, save everything for your solo . . . Now, rhythm guitar, you just play 'chks' here, see, and drums: I want a slow blues feel, with brushes, dig? Okay, here are the changes for piano and bass . . ."

Well, we understood what he was talking about and as we followed his instructions, we began to see how he felt about his music, too. He cared a lot, just the way we did, but he knew the songs a lot better and could see them differently from the way we did.

I talked it over with Ham.

"Sure, see, Eddie, he can give you a direction. A way for you to pull together that you didn't have before, kind of like the way a painter gives a painting a shape and form and the way a director gives a play its style."

"Yeah . . ." I said, "like a guide. Not pushy, or forcing his ideas on us. Like you do for me, Ham. With the way you teach piano."

"That's what I try for, Eddie. Just guide. Only this fellow knows all the instruments—"

"—so he can put all the pieces together into a whole."

"That's right. I'm glad you found him."

We all were. Because of him—Reese's brother (we started to call him Big Reese, although we *never* said "Little Reese")—our rehearsals went smoother and better than ever and we were building what we thought was an impressive repertoire.

"Well, how do you like these?" Ivy said just before Home Room one morning. It was nearly Thanksgiving and we felt we were ready to advertise, so Ivy, the best artist, had drawn some psychedelic-looking posters.

"Hey, look!" Georgie said, pointing. "You made the buffalo without his right front leg! Hey, that's really good, Ivy!"

She smiled. "Thanks. No one'll notice it except us, but I thought it should be our trademark. I was thinking of trying to get a decal of it made for my bass drum."

"The Buffalo Nickel Blues Band, Now Accepting Bookings For the Holiday Season," I read out loud.

"People will *stampede* to your party!" Georgie read. "Well . . ."

"Come on, Georgie, it's just a slogan. I put down your number, okay, Eddie?"

"Sure," I said, "but the kids know who we all are by this time."

"Yeah, well, not all of us," Georgie said. "Nobody knows Reese."

"That's true," Ivy said with a smile. "Absolutely nobody in the world knows Reese. Not even us!"

"That doesn't matter," I said. "He's good. They'll think he's a 'ringer' we brought in. A professional."

Georgie said, "Speaking of Reese, did you show him these posters yet?"

"No, he wasn't out there this morning."

Sometimes Reese was waiting for us outside of school and—sometimes he wasn't.

You couldn't talk to him about it. Anytime anyone mentioned school to Reese he just clammed

104

right up. Wouldn't even answer, not even to Shelby, so we just stopped trying. At least no matter how much Reese lacked in his life, he had something: he had the band and he had us.

The weather was getting bad, but we were pretty snug in the garage with the mattresses stopping any draft from getting through the cracks in the wood walls. To help us out even more, my mother gave us her space heater and Georgie's and Ivy's folks each donated one too, in case it really got cold. We hardly ever needed all of them, though. We were so wrapped up in practicing we hardly ever felt the cold. In fact, most of the time we were sweating! We felt pretty confident we'd get calls, *everybody* hired some kind of group for their parties during the holidays and sure enough, the day Ivy put up our posters around school, we got a phone call during practice.

"You say the Buffalo Nickel Blues Band is ready to play parties?" a voice asked.

"Yes, that's right," I answered proudly.

"Yeah, well, we'd hire buffalo *CHIPS* before we'd hire you!" Slam!

I sighed. J.D. Ettinger again.

Well, we didn't care about J.D. Ettinger and his dumb phone calls because that week we got a booking! At lunch one day, Megan McDougal asked us if we could play at a Christmas party she was giving at her house. She said she had a huge finished basement and her father said he'd give her fifty dollars for entertainment.

"Aw, that's why she asked us, Eddie," Georgie complained. "What kind of entertainment could she get for fifty dollars anyway? Boy, that's ten dollars apiece for the whole night!"

"Georgie, don't be crazy!" I told him. "Number one, it's ten dollars more than you have now and number two, this is our first real job! Not only will we get an audience, which we need, but if we do well—and how can we miss—we'll get other jobs! And just think! We're being paid for our talent, not for mowing lawns or babysitting or something like that. We're lucky, Georgie!"

"Well, yeah, I guess, when you put it that way . . ."

"Look, we're just starting out. After this, we'll be in demand!"

A real paying job. I couldn't believe it.

"Eddie, I'm so proud of you," my mother gushed. "I knew you'd make good!"

"Could they use a dancer, Eddie?" Yvonne wanted to know.

"Hush, Yvonne, you'll have your turn. This is a grownup party: seventh graders," my mother told her.

❀

"So, Eddie, you have a job," my father said.

"Uh huh."

"Good boy."

"Thanks, Pop."

"You're welcome. It's December—maybe you get enough jobs before June you can pay for your own bar mitzvah."

"Norman!" my mother cried. "Eddie is not going to pay for his own bar mitzvah, what are you talking about!"

"I'm only kidding, can't a man kid his own son?"

"You weren't kidding, Norman."

"I was kidding, I was kidding!"

"Who knows, Pop?" I said with a shrug. "Maybe we'll be so good we'll get a recording contract and I'll be able to buy you a bar mitzvah for each year of my life!"

My father intoned, "From your mouth to God's ear," and went back to his paper.

I couldn't stop thinking about the big splash we were going to make. All anyone needed was one good break and this Christmas party was going to be ours!

"Eddie," the cantor said one afternoon in chanting class. "Where is your head? It's not on the chants. What are you thinking about?"

"Christmas," I said, dreamily.

*"Christmas?"*

"I'm sorry, Cantor," I said, realizing that chanting-class-for-your-bar-mitzvah was not the place to discuss Christmas. "I mean, our band is playing a Christmas party, that's all. I was thinking about that," I explained quickly.

"Eddie, my boy, you're supposed to be thinking about the prayers I'm giving you to chant. You're supposed to be listening very carefully, so you know how it's supposed to be done, like the other boys here. The note you just sang at me you never heard from these lips. Pay attention, please."

"I will. I'm sorry."

"Christmas," the cantor said. "Oy."

Megan McDougal's party was set for the ninth of December, a Saturday night. She told Abby Proctor who told Tricia Newman who told Ivy that she was having it early in the month so there'd be time for her to get invited back to everyone's later parties. Actually, I figured the same thing for our band!

If we were even half as good as we thought we were, everyone else would want us, too.

We had a good repertoire of songs. *Spinning Wheel, You've Made Me So Very Happy,* which Georgie sang great, *More and More, God Bless the Child, I'm a King Bee, Parachute Woman*—a whole lot of stuff. I spent a lot of time wondering how we'd manage to credit Big Reese with all he'd done for us! I wondered, too, if we'd ever meet him. He was very real and alive to us, all right, but only as a voice. Every Monday at rehearsal we'd get a new tape, and it would be an arrangement for a song we'd asked for or a song Big Reese thought we should do, or some new variations on an arrangement he'd done for us before.

". . . Now here the horn acts like a chorus, you know, like background singers, just filling in around your vocalist . . . Okay, guitar, you do a lick like this, see, doo-doo-doo-waaaaaaaaa . . ."

He never used our names, even though Reese told him what they were. We even sent him photos of ourselves (Ivy's idea) that we took with my sister Yvonne's Polaroid, paying her two bucks for the privilege.

He called us by our instruments—drums, keyboard . . .

Well, I thought, maybe someday we'd get to meet, but meanwhile what we did was send him back tapes of us playing his stuff, which Reese said he thought was "all raht!"

The night of Megan's party, I had the same feeling I'd had when we were just a trio, playing at my mother's barbecue. But even more so, I think, because this was our real audience—our friends, kids our age, who'd appreciate what we were doing. And also because it seemed like they were all prepared for us! Megan blabbed all week about the "live entertainment" she'd hired—"not any old tired records, but the real thing!"

We'd already had a meeting on what to wear. Fancy costumes were out. That's what rock groups wore to call attention to themselves and as far as I was concerned, *away* from the music. We decided on straight stuff: dark suits for the guys and Ivy could wear whatever she wanted.

I met her at our front door. What she wanted to wear turned out to be a long blue dress with puffy sleeves and shoes to match.

"The girls at the party'll be formal," she said after she'd whirled around for my mother and Yvonne. "I might as well be, too."

"It's beautiful, Ivy," Yvonne breathed. "I wish I could have one just like it . . ."

"You will when you're a famous ballet dancer," I said. This was my big night. I could afford to be nice to my sister.

"Thanks, Eddie," she said, grinning at me.

"My mother made it for me," Ivy said, patting a sleeve. "She designed it herself. But I helped! I did the hem and the petticoat!"

"Gorgeous," my mother said. "I wish I knew how to sew. And imagine, Norman, she can play drums, too! Norman, what do you think of Ivy's lovely dress?"

"Very nice," my father said and my mother threw up her hands.

110

Ivy beamed and kissed my mother on the cheek.

Georgie and Shelby got to our house at the same time. Georgie's suit was dark gray and Shelby's was blue, like mine. My mother pronounced us all "very handsome."

And then Shelby noticed Ivy. "Gee . . . Ivy . . ." he said, looking her up and down. She grinned again like a little kid who was just handed a triple-dip ice cream cone.

"It's chiffon," she said softly.

"It sure is . . . nice," he said, staring at her.

"Where's Reese?" Georgie asked. "We're going to be late."

"Yeah!" I said. "Where the heck *is* Reese?"

We all looked at each other. Everyone else was right on time . . .

"He'll be here," Ivy said. "What about the instruments, do you think Megan messed around with them after we set them up?"

"She wouldn't dare," I said. "She saw how careful we were this afternoon, especially you, Ivy. She wouldn't touch anything."

"I hope not. I hope she didn't touch the cymbals, people love to crash cymbals. Anyway, I have my sticks . . ."

"Do you think we should go over there? Maybe Reese thought he was supposed to meet us *there*," Georgie said.

"He knows where we're meeting," I grumbled. "He's never been late before . . ."

My mother frowned. "Did he have anything to wear?" she asked.

"What do you mean?"

"When you all decided on suits, did Reese say anything?"

"No," I said, thinking back. "He didn't say anything."

"Well, where do you think a boy like Reese would get a suit?" my mother said with her hands on her hips.

I drew the corners of my mouth down. "I never thought about it," I said.

"Neither did I," Shelby said.

"Me, neither," from Georgie.

"Oh, boy . . ."

"You think he won't show up because he doesn't have a suit?" Ivy cried. "Oh, no! Why didn't he say something! We could have worked something out . . ."

Georgie began to pace. "He's gonna blow it for us," he muttered. "I just know it. What's everybody going to think, our first job and all—"

Ivy said, "Georgie!" and he stopped pacing.

"Georgie, you're just like my sister Rosalie," my mother said. "Calm down. Everything will be all right. We'll wait a few more minutes."

"And then what, Mrs. Levy?"

"And then we'll see. Would anyone like a cold drink?"

"Yeah, I would, Ma," I said. I was sweating a little.

112

"Me too, thanks, Mrs. Levy," Georgie said. "And could I please have a piece of bread or something?"

"How about a whole sandwich?"

"Oh, fine, that'd be great, thanks," Georgie sighed. For someone who ate like a horse whenever he got worried, Georgie should have weighed a ton.

"Come on in the kitchen," my mother said. "Shelby? Ivy?"

They said no, thanks, and sat on the couch.

Georgie was halfway through a bologna-and-cheese sandwich and I was on my second glass of milk when we heard Ivy call from the living room.

*"He's here!* Eddie!"

We all raced out of the kitchen—my mother, too—and almost knocked each other down, running around the dining-room table.

Ivy and Shelby were already standing in front of the door and when we got there we blocked the small hallway Reese was standing in. He was wearing a nondescript dark raincoat.

"Hey, move a little, willya?" he said, and as we made a path, he stepped into the living room. "Sorry I'm late," he said gruffly.

"Oh, it's okay," Georgie said quickly and Ivy laughed.

I walked up to him. "Hey, Reese. It's okay about whatever you're wearing."

"Huh?" he said.

"I mean, it's okay if you don't have a suit or anything. You can wear whatever you want. It's the music that counts."

"Yeah, well, how about this?" he said and unbuttoned the raincoat.

Ivy said, *"Wo-ow!"*

"Man!" Shelby said.

And Georgie and I just stared.

Reese was wearing the most fantastic-looking dark pin-stripe suit with what looked like a gray silk shirt and gray-and-red print tie. Of course, he was carrying his guitar. He hadn't let us take it over to McDougals' in the truck that afternoon. It never left his side. As far as I knew, he slept with it—wherever it was he slept.

"Nice suit, Reese," Georgie said, looking him over.

"It's beautiful," Ivy said with a smile.

Reese grinned. "It's a little big," he said.

"Where'd you get it?" I asked. A dumb question. I should have waited till we got away from home.

"I—borrowed—it," Reese answered slowly and smiled at me. I sighed.

"Let's go," I said. "Come on, Pop."

My father said, "Ah," as he always does when hoisting himself to his feet.

"Good luck, oh, good luck," my mother squealed as we stuffed ourselves into our coats and tried to push through the door all at the same time.

"Good luck," Yvonne called as we piled into the

114

car, with Ivy crying, "Oh, don't crowd, don't sit on my dress . . ."

I looked back and saw my mother and sister still in the doorway in the freezing December air, waving and waving at our disappearing car.

"Oh, you're late, some of the kids are here already, gee you all look so gorgeous, the instruments are just the way you put them downstairs, let's go in the kitchen for a minute," Megan said all in one breath.

"If I had her lung power I'd *really* blow a horn," Shelby whispered and Ivy and I laughed.

We followed Megan into the kitchen. Megan was wearing a long gown, too, but not as pretty as Ivy's. Hers was green and had some flowers or something dripping down the left side.

"What we'll do," she gurgled, "is wait a little longer for everyone to come and then I'll just introduce you, okay? Do you want me to introduce you by name, I mean, everyone knows your names —oh—except you—" Megan finally discovered Reese.

"Never mind our names, Megan," I said. "It'll sound better if you just say the name of the band."

"Oh, okay . . ." She was still looking at Reese. "What is it again?"

"The Buffalo Nickel Blues Band," we all said together.

116

"Oh. The Buffalo Nickel Band," she said.

"Blues!" Georgie said.

"Okay. Blues." She finally took her eyes off Reese. "Boy, I hope you guys really rock. Listen, how about helping yourself to the food now, so you can just keep playing later? It's over there—" she swept her arm toward the counters— "only try not to upset the designs, okay? We'll be taking all the platters downstairs later and I want it to look pretty."

She meant the patterns in which the caterer had placed the food on the platters. Each platter was covered with some kind of crispy yellow see-through paper, which made all the food look yellow or green. I didn't have much of an appetite and neither did Ivy, but the other guys all heaped cold cuts onto thick white paper plates and drank iced punch out of plastic glasses with decals of Christmas trees on them. I wondered where Georgie put it all.

While we were eating, other kids began to arrive.

"Oooh, listen," Ivy whispered excitedly. "There's a big crowd!"

"Megan said she asked about forty kids," I said.

"Really? Forty?"

"She said she hopes we really rock," Georgie said, stuffing a slice of bologna into his mouth. "We don't. I mean, we don't do rock. You think that'll make a difference?"

"She just meant she hopes we're good," I said. "When she hears us, she'll be happy, all right."

"Come on, you guys, finish up," Ivy said. "We ought to get down there."

"Wait a minute," Reese said, heading for the counter. "I want some more of that turkey."

When he sat down again, I leaned over the table.

"Where'd you really get the suit, Reese?" I asked him.

He looked at me. "From a friend, Eddie, don't you believe me?" He was smiling.

"No."

"Hey, thanks a lot!"

"Aw, come on, Reese, don't give me that innocent act. I just don't want to see you in any trouble."

"I won't be in any—"

"Are you all still eating?" Megan had reappeared. "It's time to go downstairs. The spotlight is on and everything!"

"Spotlight?" We all raced for the stairway to the basement.

It looked like a ballroom down there: Red and green lights were strung all over the ceiling and walls. And on a large buffet table there were little appetizers and things to eat before the real food that we had just sampled was brought downstairs. And there was another huge crystal bowl of punch.

"Wow, some set up," Ivy breathed. "And look at our instruments!"

They looked gorgeous under a little pink spotlight set into the ceiling of the room. Very professional. I was really impressed.

Kids were standing around in pretty clothes smiling at each other and at us.

"Hey, hi, Eddie. We heard your group was playing tonight."

"Yeah, hi, Rob."

"Ivy, I just love that dress!"

"Thanks, Laurie, I love yours, too. Isn't this a pretty room?"

"Ivy! Hey!" I whispered, pulling her by the arm.

"What, Eddie, what?"

"Look. Over there by the punch bowl."

"What? Who?"

"Can't you see? Look closer."

"Oh. You mean—"

"J.D. Ettinger." In a red-checked sport jacket.

"Oh . . . so what? Come on," she said. "The other guys are getting ready."

I frowned in J.D.'s direction, but he wasn't looking at me. He was helping himself to punch.

"Okay," Megan sang loudly from the middle of the room. "Here's our entertainment for the evening! The Buffalo Blues Band!"

"Buffalo *Nickel*," I said, but Megan either didn't hear me or didn't care or whatever. She and her green dress had blended back into the crowd.

"Okay," I said, sitting down at my keyboard. "Ready? One-two, one-two-three-four—"

We hit our opening chords of *Spinning Wheel,* and nothing happened! I mean *no sound!*

"Hey!" Georgie cried.

We tried again. Nothing.

Reese said, "What the—"

"What happened to the amps?" I cried, leaping up.

There were some nervous giggles from the kids.

"What's going on?" Megan asked, reappearing again. She reminded me of a blinking Christmas light.

"I don't know. There's something wrong with the amplification. Maybe the socket's bad. Can we plug in somewhere else?"

"There's nothing wrong with the socket," Megan said. "And it was working this afternoon when your father tested it." This was said angrily to Ivy, as if it were her father's fault. Or hers.

"Well, we're not getting any sound!" Georgie said.

Shelby said, "Just a minute," and put down his horn. He walked over to the back of Reese's big amp and knelt down. Then he shook his head and stood up.

"What is it, Shel?" I asked.

"The fuse is missing," he said and went over to check mine. "Yours, too, Eddie. The fuses are missing. Look, the cap's gone."

The cap is about a half-an-inch in diameter and when you push it in and turn it, a fuse about an inch long comes out with the cap. It's easy to take out. Easy. But impossible to find a replacement for on a Saturday night. My mind was moving like a Concorde jet. Our fuses are gone, we can't play, we have to replace the fuses, J.D. Ettinger's father could replace them if J.D. called and said it was an emergency, J.D. could—wait a minute, wait a minute—our fuses! How could they disappear like that in the first place? Someone had to take them! Someone who knew about amps and knew exactly where the fuse box was and how it worked . . .

"Where's Ettinger?" I barked.

"Listen, what's going on here, Eddie?" Megan whined. "Are you going to play or not?"

"Megan, look, someone's stolen our fuses! We can't get any sounds out of our electric instruments unless the amplifiers are working and they can't work without fuses. Now who was around here today, messing with our instruments?"

She looked blank, then angry again. "No one! Who would do something like that!"

"Was J.D. Ettinger here?"

"No. Why him?"

"Because he was the one who took them, Megan."

"Come on, Eddie," Ivy said, coming over to me. "You can't say that. We don't have any proof."

"Do you really need proof, Ivy? Where is he, anyway? I bet he skipped out!"

"Did you call me?" J.D. was suddenly standing next to me, all innocence and wide eyes.

"Okay, J.D., that was a lousy trick. Let's have the fuses back," I said.

"What fuses?"

"What fuses?" I mimicked derisively. "The ones you took out of our amps. Those fuses. Look, J.D., come on. A joke's a joke, but that's enough. It's not fair to Megan and it's not fair to us. So let's have them. Now."

"I don't know what you're talking about."

"Is that so? You don't know what I'm talking about?"

He shook his head.

"Okay, J.D., if you're so innocent, then help us out here. Call your father and have him get us some new ones from his store. He'd do that for you, won't he? My father will even go over to pick them up."

"My father will go," Megan said, sounding a little hysterical. "I promised live music, Eddie—"

"Well, you'll have it, if J.D. here just cooperates."

But J.D. just widened his eyes and kept shaking his head. "My father isn't here," he said, every word dripping honey. "He and my mother went to a Broadway show tonight. They won't be back until late. I'd really like to help you, Eddie, but there's not a thing I can do."

122

The only live music that night was Shelby's horn. He'd gotten awfully good at improvising and he played some nice solo stuff, even some songs that sounded really good, but not exactly your basic dance music. Megan ran upstairs crying and stayed there for about an hour. Her mother came down finally and asked if I could play Christmas carols on the upstairs piano and I said, "Sure," so the party moved up there and we all sang carols until it was time to eat the cold cuts and other stuff.

I didn't think Megan's party was ruined, but she did, and our first "big chance" went right down the tubes.

"Do you really think it was Ettinger?" Reese asked while we were waiting for Ivy's father to pick us up with our stuff.

"I know it was," I said.

"I think it was, too," Georgie said. "I'd bet on it. Did you see those baby blues he was flashing when you put it to him?"

"He did it all right," I said.

"Well, then, don't worry about it. I'll get him," Reese said.

"Don't," I warned. "You've got enough trouble with your suit."

Reese grinned. "I told you, the suit's borrowed!"

I felt the material on his sleeve. "Listen, Reese," I said seriously, "we could have lent you something, or worked something else out. You didn't have to steal a suit."

"I didn't steal it!"

Ivy's father arrived then and helped us load the truck. The party was still going on but we had no reason to stay. Megan refused to say goodbye to us, but her parents did and told us how sorry they were. We said we were a lot sorrier, and we were.

Ivy's father felt awful, too.

"I'm sorry, kids," he said. "You waited so long for this. It's a big letdown, I know how you feel. Our 'Grand Opening' for the grocery store was delayed ten days. Had to take down the streamers and eat all the party food ourselves. Remember, Ivy?"

Ivy answered by bursting into tears and Mr. Sunday put his arms around her there in the front seat of the truck.

"Aw, come on, babe," he said softly. "There'll be lots of other times . . ."

"I'll get him," Reese muttered in the back. "Oh-ho, you watch, I'll get him."

Ivy sniffled. I had to admire her, the way she held it in until we were out of Megan McDougal's house. I knew she wanted to cry. There were a couple of times I felt like it myself.

Shelby leaned forward and touched Ivy's shoulder. "It's okay, Ivy," he said softly. "We're going to be heard yet, you'll see. And anyway, you were the—" he stopped.

Ivy blotted her eyes on her coat sleeve and turned around.

"The what?" she asked.

"I was just going to say you had the prettiest dress," Shelby said lamely.

"Thank you," Ivy said and tried to smile.

"I'll just bet you did," her father said. "Even the boys noticed!"

After that there was an embarrassed silence until Reese leaned toward the front and tapped Ivy's father on the shoulder.

"Hey, Mr. Sunday, could you make one stop for me along the way?"

"Sure, Reese, no problem. Where are you going?"

Reese directed him to the northern part of Centerin City, where they were building some new co-ops and high risers. Fancy buildings, with doormen and awnings. Reese kept directing Mr. Sunday while Georgie and Shelby and I kept looking at each other and shrugging our shoulders.

"That one! That finished one, over there on the corner," Reese called and Mr. Sunday pulled up at the curb. "Can you wait? I'll be only five minutes!" And Reese bounded out of the truck and over to the doorman where he seemed to be giving his name or something. The rest of us in the truck must have looked so funny to anyone passing by because all of us, including Mr. Sunday, had moved over to the curb side and had our noses pressed tight to the glass, staring at Reese. We must

125

have looked like one of those cars full of clowns at the circus.

To our amazement, the doorman nodded at Reese, pressed a button, spoke into the phone, and directed Reese inside.

Ten minutes later, he was back, in his own clothes—jeans, dirty windbreaker and wool cap. The doorman gave him a different look as he walked out.

"Thanks a lot, Mr. Sunday. Hope I didn't keep you waiting too long," Reese said as he climbed in.

"Perfectly okay, Reese, no problem."

Reese leaned back and stared out the window.

Georgie got dropped off and then Shelby. It was the first time I'd seen Shelby's house. It was a beauty—two big stories; brick on the lower half and then the upper half was a light color with dark-colored wood outlines. That kind of house has a name—Tudor, I think.

All the lights were on outside.

"Uh, I guess my folks are up," Shelby said.

"I guess they wanted to hear about the party," Mr. Sunday offered.

Just then the front door opened and a woman waved at the truck.

"Uh oh," Shelby murmured.

"That your mother?" I asked. "In the doorway waving?"

"Yeah . . . Um, Ivy, can I leave my trumpet with you? Pick it up tomorrow? Would it be okay?"

"Sure."

"Thanks. Night, everybody. Thanks a lot for the lift, Mr. Sunday." He slammed the door of the truck and Mr. Sunday began to pull out of the driveway.

"What was that all about?" Reese asked, nudging me.

I shrugged. "Another mystery from the Mystery Man," I said.

"Why didn't he take his horn in the house?"

"I dunno. Maybe it's contagious." I tried to look at Ivy's face but it was hard with her sitting in the front and it was dark, besides. "Ivy?" I said tentatively. "You know why Shelby didn't take his horn in?"

I could see her shoulders shrug. "Guess he had his reasons," she said, just as her father half-turned toward the back.

"Where you getting off, Reese?" Mr. Sunday asked.

"At Eddie's," Reese answered, and then whispered to me, "Okay with you?"

"Why not?"

"Don't mind taking you anywhere, Reese . . ."

"Thanks, Mr. Sunday, but I'm gonna stay with Eddie."

We got off at my house, my keyboard and I and Reese and his guitar and our fuseless amps. I was glad Reese was going to be there. It would be hard explaining about the party to my parents and now Reese'd be there to pick up the slack.

"Oh, no! Your fuses?" my mother wailed. "You

really think it was the Ettinger boy? I can't believe it!"

"I'm sure it was J.D., Ma, I just couldn't prove it. Anyway, it's over now . . ."

"You poor kids!"

My father shook his head sadly. "Eddie, into each life—"

"I know, Pop, a little rain must fall."

"It's not the last job in the world, Eddie."

"Gig, Pop."

"Gig?"

"Gig. That means job."

"If gig means job why not say job?"

"Because you say gig, Norman," my mother said.

"Gig, job—it's not the last one in the world, Eddie," my father said.

"What's a gigjob?"

"Yvonne, what are you doing up?" my mother asked as she noticed my sister sitting on the stairs.

"I woke up. I wanted to hear about Eddie's job."

My mother and father and Reese and I all cried, "Gig!"

"Huh?" Yvonne said.

"Aw, we got sabotaged, Yvonne. A kid stole our fuses and we couldn't play."

"That's terrible!" Yvonne said.

"Terrible," my mother repeated. Then she stood up. "But your father's right. It's not the last—"

"*Gig!*"

"—gig in the world, so cheer up and wait for the

128

next one. Yvonne, go get the extra sleeping bag in the bottom of your closet and bring it into Eddie's room for Reese, okay?"

"Okay . . ." Yvonne yawned.

"And then go back to sleep. You hear?"

"Uh huh . . ."

❧

When the light was out and we were in bed and bag, I sleepily brought up Reese's suit again.

"Listen, Reese," I said, "I'm sorry I didn't believe you—that your suit wasn't stolen."

Reese laughed. "I didn't say it wasn't stolen, Eddie," he said.

"You did!"

"No, I said *I* didn't *steal* it! There's a big difference!"

"What?"

"My brother has this cellmate who knows these people. They fence things. Like, one week it's meat, y'know? Big chunks of cow, sides of beef, okay? The next week it could be women's pocketbooks. Real leather, lizard skin, satin, whatever. Next week they've got TVs or stereos, or quartz watches or something."

"And this week it's—"

"Men's suits. Best quality. Wool. Sharkskin. Anyway, it's not this week, it's next week. I got the jump on it. I had my pick."

"So you went to their apartment—"

129

"Their suite of apartments. And I changed there. I had to get the suit back before morning, though. That was the deal. My brother fixed it for me. I don't know what he had to do for it, but you can bet it cost him!"

"Yeah, but Reese—"

"I didn't steal it, Eddie. Somebody else did!"

I sighed. Rehabilitating Reese wasn't going to be easy.

# .10.

A week later, I got a call from J.D. Ettinger. I nearly hung up when I heard his voice, but he stopped me by yelling, "I got you another party!"

"Huh?"

"I apologize," he said very slowly, "for the dirty trick I played on you at Megan's party." There was a mumbling voice in the background. I couldn't hear what it said, but J.D. went on. "I took the fuses out while all the kids were taking off their coats and walking around and getting punch and stuff." The background voice mumbled again. "And to prove how sorry I am I'm having a Christmas party of my own and inviting you to play." Then, though he must have cupped the mouthpiece, I heard him say distinctly, "There. Is that enough?" And back into the phone. "So is it okay now, Eddie?"

"What's the catch, J.D.?" I asked, still suspicious.

"There isn't any catch. The party's Friday night. Informal."

"I don't believe you."

J.D. cupped the mouthpiece again and mumbled something. And then someone else got on.

"It's legit, Eddie. Tell the others," the new voice said and hung up. It was Reese.

❀

"How'd you do it?" we asked Reese at our next rehearsal.

"You wouldn't believe me."

"We would," Georgie said. "Tell us."

"I'm telling you, you won't believe me."

"*Try* us!" Ivy cried.

"Okay, but you won't believe it. I cornered him on his way out of school. I told him if he didn't come with me I'd break his skinny neck right there behind a bush."

"And he went?"

"Are you kidding? He was shaking like a leaf."

"Well, where did you take him?"

"I took him home. Where I live. With my sister."

It was the first time Reese had mentioned his home. Or a sister, for that matter. But we didn't interrupt him.

"My sister works so she wasn't there. I locked Ettinger and me in her room. She has a room of her own, I sleep on the couch in the other room. Then I turned on my brother's tape recorder and I made Ettinger play."

"Play! Ettinger can't play!"

"He can play five simple little riffs, real slow, he has to figure them out."

132

"Well, that's not playing . . ."

"You're telling me! He can't even get most of 'em right! So I taped him, squeaking and groaning, and I made him sing."

"Sing!"

"Yeah, sing to his chords. Then I hooked the machine up to the amp, see, I plugged the output of the tape recorder into the input of the amp and turned up the amp volume real loud and played it back to him."

"Wait a minute, you played back the tape you made of him playing and singing?"

"If you could call it 'playing and singing', yeah, I played it back in his face, so loud I'm surprised you guys didn't hear it all the way over here. My ears are shattered, I hope I can still play."

"You mean you stayed in there with him?"

"I *had* to, otherwise he could've just turned it off. Can you just hear it? A tape of *Ettinger playing?* Over and over and over and over and *loud?*"

"Torture!"

"Torture, yeah. For me but also for him. I kept yelling, *You wanna play in a band, Ettinger? You want people to hear this? Listen, Ettinger, listen!*"

"That was awful to do to him," Ivy giggled.

"Yeah, awful," Georgie added.

"I think it was brilliant," Shelby said and smiled.

"Well, he deserved it," I said.

"I told him he'd have to stay in that room and listen to himself unless he thought of some way to make it up to us for Megan's party. And he did. He thought of having a party himself."

❀

J.D. Ettinger lived in the same part of town as Megan McDougal and his house was just as nice, and decorated nicely, too. The differences were that there were a lot fewer kids at J.D.'s—I guess around twenty, maybe less—and the food wasn't catered. J.D.'s mother made it all. It was better than Megan's gigantic spread. And the five of us dressed in white shirts and jeans so clothes weren't any problem.

We introduced ourselves instead of having J.D. do it and began to do our stuff. We felt great. At last we had an audience, an outlet, people to share with. We'd worked so hard, were ready to go on working, but now there were other people to enjoy our work. It made us so happy, we didn't notice that our audience reaction was kind of strange. When I stood up to introduce our third song, Craig deVechio yelled out, "Hey, what song is *that!* I never heard of any of that stuff you're playing!"

Megan McDougal sniffed, "Me neither."

"Come on, Eddie, do Kiss!"

"Lynyrd Skynyrd!"

"Blondie!"

They were all yelling at us to do the songs of their favorite rock groups.

"Listen, we wanted to do something different,"

I called out. "This is good music. How about the horn and stuff, don't you like the sound?"

There were what the movies call crowd noises.

"You play okay," Whitman Jones said, "but we want rock. Can't you rock?"

I sighed. We started to do the four or five rock tunes we'd worked on. This wasn't Big Reese's stuff and it wasn't as good, but this was what the kids seemed to want. Shelby smiled a little sheepishly, put away his horn and went to join the party. When Ivy and Georgie and Reese and I finished the stuff we'd rehearsed, we improvised the rest. It wasn't hard. The kids danced, they didn't complain but they didn't think we were all that great and I didn't either. Our hearts weren't in it. We had worked hard to do something different and these kids wanted the same old stuff!

"These kids have no taste," I grumbled as we began to pack up.

Ivy said, "Yeah, they wouldn't appreciate something good if it ran up and pinched 'em."

Georgie leaned against the wall. "So what?" he said. "So what, maybe we learned something."

"What?"

"We are good musicians, right? And good musicians can play anything. So if the kids want rock then we'll play good rock. Why not?"

Ivy and I frowned.

"Rock ain't good," Reese growled. "Blues is where it's at, man."

"There's plenty of rock that's pretty good," Georgie argued.

"Yeah, but Georgie," I said, "we started out originally not doing rock so that we could be different. Now that we've learned so much from trying new things, how could we go backwards?"

"To be a popular group and get gigs," Georgie answered.

"Shelby, what do you think?" Ivy said.

"Come on, Ivy, you can't ask Shelby that!" Reese said. "If this band goes rock, then it's out one horn player!"

"Oh, that's right!" Ivy cried and covered her mouth with her fingers.

Shelby gave us that little smile of his and shrugged.

"I just don't think it would be right to give up everything we worked for and like so much," I said.

"Hey, Ivy's father's here!" J.D. called, trotting down the stairs. We began to pick up our stuff.

J.D. peered at us. "Reese didn't say I had to pay you, too," he whined.

"Naw, you don't," I told him. "You paid us by having the party and giving us the chance to play. Too bad we bombed."

J.D. jerked his body to attention. "Bombed! You're crazy! You were great!"

"Say what?" Reese said from under his eyebrows.

"Well, I *mean!*" J.D. said with a wave of his fingers. "Anyone could tell even from the rock stuff that you guys were real musicians. But that stuff you were playing in the beginning—that was fantastic!"

"You really dug that, huh?" Reese said.

"Oh, yeah!" J.D. answered earnestly. "You were right, Eddie, I guess I wasn't good enough to play with you."

Ivy dug her fingernails into my arm so I wouldn't laugh.

"Yeah, well, we've been playing a long time, J.D.," I said, kindly, I thought.

"Yeah, it's okay, kid," Reese said to J.D. "We're even now."

"You really liked our blues stuff, huh, J.D.?" Shelby asked.

"Oh, yeah! And you know what? I still think there's a place for me with your band."

"Come on, J.D. don't start again—"

"No, no, I don't mean playing!"

"Not playing?"

"Not playing."

"Doing what, then, caddying our axes?" Georgie said, looking down at J.D. Georgie was about a head taller.

"No, not that. I'm not a brawn-person, I'm a brain-person. You don't have a manager, do you?"

Ivy said, "Huh?"

Shelby beamed. "A manager! No, we don't, do we, Eddie?"

"No," I said. "We don't have a manager, J.D." I

smiled. That little hustler would probably make a good manager, I thought—if he could find anyone who liked what we did. Maybe seventh-graders were too young. Maybe high-schoolers . . .

"—about it?" J.D. was saying.

I shook my head. "What, J.D.?"

"I said, how about it? Can I? Be your manager?"

"I bet you'd make a good manager, J.D." I said, meaning it. "And I'm glad you like our music. But your guests weren't that crazy about it, so even if you can get us bookings, I don't know if we'll be liked that much . . . Not that I want to stop working, but—"

"Not to worry," J.D. said, sounding managerial already. "Maybe the kids aren't your audience. *I'll* find your audience."

"So, Eddie! A long face *again?*"

I worked up a smile. "Hi, Ma."

"What's wrong?"

"Nothing . . ."

"Eddie, your mother you can't fool. What happened, the fuses again?"

"Naw . . ."

"Reese all right?"

"Fine . . ."

"You remembered all the notes?"

I smiled. "Yeah . . ."

"Well?"

138

"Aw, Ma . . . I just want to be by myself a little while. Okay?"

"Okay," she said, nodding. I went upstairs to my room, passing my father who was sitting up in bed reading.

"Hello, Eddie."

"Hello, Pop."

"Okay?"

"Okay . . ."

"Good night."

"Night, Pop."

I really appreciated that my mother cared about me enough to rake me over the coals and I really appreciated that my father cared about me enough not to.

Within one minute, there was a soft rap on my door.

"Pssst! Eddie! How about a piece of cake?"

"No, thanks, Ma."

A stage whisper next to the crack in the door: "What?"

"I said *no,*" I stage-whispered back.

"But it's devil's food. Marshmallow icing."

"No!"

"What?"

*"No cake!"*

She walked in with a plateful.

"Ma, I said I didn't want any."

"I couldn't understand you through the door. Here. Eat it. You don't have to worry about pimples yet and fat you're not."

"Thanks," I said, digging in.

"You're welcome."

"You know," I mumbled with my mouth full, "the kids really want to hear rock. They don't like our style, Ma."

"It's good music," my mother said.

"I know, I know. But they want rock. They want to dance to their own familiar beat. Georgie thinks we should play what they want."

"What do you think?"

"I don't want to, but I don't know how we can work if we don't."

"Hmph."

"What are we supposed to do, Ma?"

She touched my hand—the one that was holding the plate, not the one with the fork that was shoveling cake into my mouth. "What I think is, every week I shlep my extraordinarily talented son way out to Jefferson to study with an expert. And it seems to me that it wouldn't hurt to get some expert advice from this expert. Hm?"

"Ask Ham, you mean, huh? Yeah, that's a good idea, Ma."

"I thought you'd run up against something like this," Ham said, leaning with one elbow on the top of his piano.

"You did? How come you never said anything?"

"Well, because I'm not a fortune-teller. I'm not

about to predict your problems in advance. But you're not the first, you know, to discover that the art he loves may not go over big with the world!"

"You mean, like—"

"I mean, like Gauguin, Bizet, Mozart, listen, you want me to go on? It'd take up all your lesson time!"

"Are you comparing me with *Mozart?*" I asked, impressed.

Ham sat down next to me on the bench. "Look, Eddie," he said, "this is an age-old artistic decision you have to make here. Do you want to play the kind of music you like, or do you want to be 'cool with the kids'?"

"Geez, I—"

"Now, look, there's nothing wrong with being popular. It's a lot of fun, but if you have to compromise your artistic temperament to do it, then you have to decide if it's worth it or not . . . You know, I used to be a lawyer."

"Yeah, I know."

"I had a good job with CBS. I was very popular. Had a lot of friends."

"What did they say when you quit?" I asked.

"They thought I fell out of my tree. They thought I was crazy."

"Because you wanted to teach piano? And play music?"

"Yep. I don't make anywhere near as much money as I did before."

"But this makes you happier," I said.

"Are you kidding? I haven't worn a suit in two years! Yeah, kid, this makes me a lot happier, but what I'm saying is, what's right for one person may not be right for another. You might be happier wearing the suit. Eh, Eddie?"

I had to get to everybody, especially Georgie! I knew how *I* felt, how I'd always felt without realizing it, but I had to know about *them*. Just as Ham said, it was an individual decision. But me—I wouldn't have a good time if I were doing something simply to be popular. And if I wasn't going to have a good time, then why do it at all!

I stayed up a long time that night, thinking about what Ham said and how I could talk to the band about it. Finally I fell asleep, dreaming that I was Mozart in a white powdered wig, playing *Blues Power* at a party for lawyers at CBS Records.

What was weirder than that was, at the time I never really got to talk to anybody about artistic integrity vs. popularity. Like a lot of things you plan, the road curves a little bit and you find yourself going through a different territory.

The next day was Thursday and things were pretty slack at school because Friday was the last day before Christmas vacation and not much work

142

was being done. A lot of the classes were having parties.

I looked all over for Ivy and Georgie before lunch, but I never saw them in the halls. When I raced into the cafeteria at lunch time I saw Ivy and Shelby at a table by themselves, way in the back. I almost knocked down a kid getting over there.

I plopped my lunch bag down on the table and sat next to Ivy.

"Hi!" I said quickly. "I talked to Ham yesterday and we got into this real—" I stopped talking suddenly when I saw their faces. Ivy had this look that you'd probably wear if you'd been watching a great movie and suddenly the projector broke down.

"Did I interrupt something?" I asked.

"Oh, no!"

"No!"

"Because if I did, I mean, it can wait until practice—"

"No, we were just talking," Ivy said casually and she smiled at Shelby.

I guess I'd have been pretty dumb not to catch on. Ivy and Shelby liked each other. Ivy had always been the one I liked to talk to and confide in, but I guess when you have someone you like as a boyfriend or girlfriend, maybe they're the ones you confide in. I don't know because I've never really had a girlfriend, just a girl—*friend,* which is different. But I felt right then that someone else had taken my place with Ivy, even though Shelby was a friend, too.

So I got up and said, "It's okay, it can wait till later," and went looking for some other kids to eat with.

❈

We never got to play that afternoon because we were all talking.

"I still think we should put at least *some* rock tunes in our repertoire," Georgie insisted. "It sure wouldn't hurt."

"I like what we've been doing," Ivy said firmly. I wondered if she really meant it or was just saying it so Shelby could stay with the group.

I finally told them all about my conversation with Ham, and Reese kept punctuating everything I said with "Yeah!" and "Right on!"

And in the middle of it all, J.D. appeared in the garage wrapped in a green down jacket and six-foot scarf.

"Ettinger, you look like you're on a leash," Reese laughed.

J.D. ignored him. "Got a booking for you," he said.

The discussion was forgotten. "What is it?" we cried.

"My father has a New Year's Eve day party at his store every year. It's in the afternoon and it's for his employees and their families and other people he deals with at the store. He always opens the main studio in the back for it. And he wants the Buffalo Nickels to play."

"Really?"

"The kind of thing we do? Blues?"

"Uh huh. He heard you at our house. He thinks you're terrific!"

J.D. Ettinger's father owned a music store and he thought we were terrific! That was just the shot in the arm we needed. We practiced harder than ever, and after Friday, we had days to work, too. Somehow we managed to get our Christmas and Chanukah shopping done and all our regular chores, too, like Ivy at her store and me with my father's envelope-stuffing, and we even managed to learn two new arrangements that Big Reese sent us.

For presents, Ivy made little black-and-white sketches of each of us playing our instruments. I gave her a little pin in the shape of a drum. And my mother knitted wool hats for each band member and added a warm scarf for Reese, whom she said always looked as if he were freezing to death.

Funny, but I wasn't nervous for the Ettinger party. Georgie ate lunch at my house and then he ate lunch at the store, so I knew he was nervous, but I was feeling pretty good. Ivy arrived with

146

Shelby and when I smiled at her she winked back. Reese got there alone and on time, wearing my mother's scarf. J.D. started to say something about *his* leash, but chickened out.

The five of us hung around together during the party. The guests were all grownups except for the younger kids of the Ettinger employees and after we set up our instruments there wasn't much for us to do until we were introduced.

"Okay, kids, you ready?" Mr. Ettinger said finally.

"Oh, yeah!"

"The Buffalo Nickel Blues Band, right?"

"You got it!"

"Okay, who's the drummer?"

"I am!" Ivy piped up.

"Good. You give us a little drum roll, okay?"

Ivy sat down and went *BRRRRRRRRRRRRR-RRR—CRASH!* and the big room was suddenly quiet.

"Ladies and Gentlemen," Mr. Ettinger announced, "I want you to relax and enjoy the amazing, the swinging, the unusual—Buffalo Nickel Blues Band of our own Centerin City!"

My face felt flushed and my stomach was jumping. I nodded the beat and we were on, doing *And When I Die,* starting with Shelby's muted horn and Georgie coming in with his vocal and Ivy's drums, and then Reese and me, with a bouncy, rinky-dink plink-plunkin' solo. Boy, was it happy!

147

The guests clapped in rhythm and they were all grinning from ear to ear, just like we were, and we played for nearly forty-five minutes straight! It was wonderful!

When we stopped, all of us sweating with the work and the excitement, the guests came up to us and nearly pushed us over our instruments.

"Terrific!"

"Wonderful!"

"Never heard kids play this music, and so well!"

"I just love that horn! Say, aren't you the Powell boy?"

I looked over, beaming, at Shelby, but his face suddenly fell apart.

"Uh . . ." he said.

"Aren't you Dr. Powell's boy?" the man asked again, and Ivy said quickly, "Did you really like the horn, sir? It makes our sound, don't you think?" and the man forgot Shelby and said that yes, it certainly did.

Someone said, "We'll be hearing this band again!" and as they began to move away, some of my excitement faded. Puzzled, I kept staring at Shelby.

Ivy moved close to him. "Don't worry," she said. "He didn't connect anything. Don't worry, Shelby . . ."

A woman in a black dress came up to Reese and me.

"I just loved you kids," she gurgled.

"Thanks," I said.

"I'm having a cocktail party Friday night. A sort of after-New-Year's celebration. Would your band play?"

I turned to the others. "Ivy? Shel? Hey, Georgie? Did you hear that? Friday night okay?"

Georgie cried, "Sure!" and Reese nodded happily and I said, "You bet! Where do you live?" The woman began to pull some paper and a pencil out of her purse and while she was writing down her address, I saw Shelby hastily putting his trumpet into its case. I took the address, checked the time and thanked the lady, trying to do it all and beat Shelby to the door at the same time.

"Shel! Wait a minute!"

"Eddie, I—"

"No, wait, please—"

Ivy was there and Georgie and Reese came over, too.

"What's wrong?" J.D. asked. He was always "appearing."

Shelby sagged against the wall. "Hey, J.D., is there a place where we could talk for a second? Away from the party?"

"Me, too?" J.D. asked plaintively.

Shelby sighed. "Yeah, you, too," he said finally.

"The office," J.D. said and led the way.

When the door was closed behind us, I said, "Shelby, just what *is* it with you?"

Shelby rolled his eyes. Then he took a deep breath. We waited.

"I didn't mean to make this a big deal," he be-

149

gan. "The thing is, my parents don't know I play in a band."

"They don't?" Reese asked.

"Where did they think you were, then?" I asked. "When we played at Megan's and then at—"

"At a party, that's all. They thought I went to a party. Which I did."

"But what about practice every day? Where do they think you go then?"

"My parents work. My father's a doctor and my mother works as a receptionist and assistant at his office. She doesn't get home till a little after five—"

"And that's why you have to be home at five," I finished. "But I don't get it. Why can't you tell them you play in a—"

"Eddie, would you please just let him finish?" Ivy said and I shut up.

"I'm a classical musician," Shelby said.

"He's a prodigy," Ivy said proudly. "A genius." Shelby shook his head, embarrassed.

"A for-real genius?" Reese asked.

"The thing is, when my mother comes in that door around five, I've got to be in my room making classical sounds. I've studied for years. It's going to be my career."

"Yeah, but wouldn't they be proud you do other things, too?" Georgie asked.

"No way. The band is like my secret life. I wanted to do it. When I saw your sign on the bulletin board, Eddie, I knew I had to try. I never played this kind of music before, I never played in a group. I wanted to learn and I wanted to be— you know—" he shrugged.

"With regular kids," Ivy finished.

"Yeah. When I play the parties . . . I lower the horn from a window on a string."

"That's why you freaked when your mother was waiting for you. After Megan's."

"That's why I gave the horn to Ivy. Did you guys ever hear of Bubs Huggins?"

"Bubs Huggins, yeah!" Reese cried. "Famous Dixieland cornet man!"

"He was my grandfather."

"No kidding!" Reese whistled.

"No kidding. But don't ever mention him to my mother. See, he was famous, all right. He was so famous he never knew his family was alive. At least that's the way my mother tells it. Spent half his life on a train, the other half in a saloon. My mother says she remembers hanging onto his leg, him dragging her halfway down the road as he was pulling out of town again, with her crying and wailing for him not to go away."

"Man," Georgie said.

"He loved music. It was all he knew. Oh, he wasn't so famous while he was alive except with other musicians. They all knew him, of course. But it was after he died that he began to be appreciated by jazz-lovers all over."

"Guess your mother didn't appreciate him, though, huh?" J.D. said.

Shelby shook his head. "When I was this high and started playing toy horns, flutes, recorders, begging for a horn that went wah-wah-waaaaah, she was pretty upset."

"But she let you study . . ."

"Finally. Classical. It was her compromise. Serious music is different, she says. Serious music's for high-class respectable people, not some wino calling up in the middle of the night with an offer of two one-nighters in Kansas City and Independence. And grabbing your bag and your horn and making it to the fleabag depot in time for the Midnight Special, dragging your kid down the road . . ."

"She thinks you'd grow up to be like that if you just played in a band with your friends?" I asked.

"I don't know, Eddie . . . I guess so. You know how people are when they have a thing about something. I just never wanted to see what would happen if she ever found out, that's all."

"Well, why didn't you tell us?" I wanted to know.

Shelby shrugged. "I don't know. I didn't mean to make everything so secretive, I really didn't think it would be a big deal. And I liked the 'secret life' idea, I guess. But listen, when that guy asked me if I were Dr. Powell's son I figured, boy, that's it!"

We all looked at our shoes for a while.

152

"Shelby, we got a gig Friday night," I said.

"And I got you another one," J.D. said. "For the week after. This is your audience, guys! For your music, these are your people! We found 'em!"

But Shelby kept shaking his head. "I can't. I can't play for grownups. My father's a doctor, *somebody's* going to know me! Look, don't you think I want to keep playing with you? This music—do you know I play my exercises differently now as a result of learning blues? It's a whole new technique of practicing—it's been great for me!"

"Shelby, you don't have to stop," Ivy said. "We can take all kinds of precautions."

"Precautions?"

"Sure. First of all, don't wear your glasses."

"I can't see without my glasses."

"You don't have to see to play trumpet. And you can wear a slouch hat, one that pulls over your eyes a little. We'll say it's your trademark. In fact, we'll *each* wear one!"

We laughed. "Good idea," I cried.

"And then, we'll go in first. Before you. And we'll mingle with the crowd . . ."

"And find out who everybody's doctor is?" Shelby laughed.

"We'll just case the joint," Reese said.

"And with the hat, and no glasses—"

"Maybe I should wear whiteface!" Shelby laughed again.

"They won't know you, Shel," I said. "The

chances are one in a million you'll run into anyone you know."

Shelby sighed. "I really don't want to quit this group," he said.

"Oh, good!" Ivy cried.

Everyone was glad to get out of the stuffy office, glad about the way things turned out. As Ivy was going through the door, I pulled her aside.

"Isn't it great, Eddie?" she asked.

"Yeah, sure," I said. "But Ivy, I have to ask you something."

"What?"

"Did you know all along? About Shelby?"

"Not the whole time, Eddie," she said.

"Just when you started liking each other, huh?"

She looked down. "I couldn't say anything when he asked me not to, Eddie. I didn't want to keep secrets from you, but it wasn't my secret, it was Shelby's."

"I understand."

"Besides, it's hard to go around telling your friends you're a genius."

"Is he really?"

"Yeah. He studies with Gianni Larzo and someday the world will hear about him."

"The world, huh?"

"You're not mad at me, are you, Eddie? We still friends?"

"Oh, yeah," I said. "Oh, sure! Hey, Ivy, weren't we great today?"

# 12.

The first adult party we played was a gas! We all wore hats and four of us and Ivy's brother went into the party first, leaving Shelby outside in the bushes, while Raymond helped us set up our stuff.

"Look for black people first," Shelby said. "That would put us closer to home."

"Okay," Georgie said. "And if no black people then start asking around who knows a good internist?"

Shelby groaned.

"Stop worrying!" Ivy said. "With that hat on, *Raymond* barely recognized you."

"Okay, okay . . ."

It wasn't a big party, but when it was time for us to play, Shelby slunk in through the basement door behind his hat.

"I can't see," he said. "Where are the stairs?"

Ivy took his arm. "Can you see my feet? Just look at them and keep walking. We'll get you upstairs."

"I have to put my head back when I play. My hat'll fall off!"

"It won't. Don't put your head back so far."

Shelby couldn't see, but he could play and it seemed to me that the party was a huge success. The hostess shouted requests and some of the guests sang along and everybody stamped their feet and clapped on the rhythm tunes.

"Aren't they cute, Ralph?" I overheard some woman say. "Why don't we have them play for Martha's birthday dinner next month?"

I tugged at my own slouch hat and smiled.

Raymond came back at ten-thirty with J.D. to pick up our stuff. J.D. walked right up to the surprised hostess and shook her hand.

"Glad you liked my people, here," he said. "Here's our card, I hope you'll pass the word along."

Reese whistled low through his teeth. Shelby pulled his hat lower.

"Where'd you get a *card?*" I whispered to J.D.

"I asked your father to make them up, Eddie. I told him I'd pay him from our first gig. Off the top."

I glared at him.

"It's good business, Eddie!" he insisted. He handed me one of the cards. It had a small picture of a buffalo nickel with a little half-note next to it. And it had our name, of course, and J.D. Ettinger's telephone number.

I was about to say something when I saw the

hostess passing the card around to her guests and smiling.

"What a good idea," someone said.

"I've got them first!" someone else said. "For Martha's birthday!"

They were arguing over us! They wanted us!

When Megan McDougal had asked us to play for her Christmas party, I was excited. I thought we'd found our real audience—our friends. But I was wrong. You had to be a little bit older to appreciate what we were doing and so *here* was our real audience!

These folks were older and they liked not only the music, but the fact that younger kids were playing it—kids who didn't grow up with this music, the way they had.

J.D. had been right. There was a place for us after all and we didn't have to compromise!

I turned back to where the kids had been, but the only ones left were Reese and Georgie, putting their coats on. Shelby had been the first one out the door, along with Raymond, carrying Ivy's drums.

J.D.'s phone jumped off the hook after that party. I had to hand it to him, he hustled for us. The cards were a good idea, and not only did he hand them out, he had a little stack of them next to the cash register in his father's store. It seemed we had gigs at least one night every single week-end! Big Reese was kept busy in his cell, or wher-ever it was he worked, and we kept learning and practicing and playing. And having fun!

❖

A Saturday.

"Shelby, don't you think you can come in now without worrying?"

"No, now you go in first and look around, like we agreed."

"But, Shelby, the hat was good enough to begin with. Now with those weird shades, your mother could be right in there and she wouldn't know you!"

Reese had bought Shelby a pair of dark glasses that were so large they could have shaded the eyes of an elephant. But Shelby felt comfortable with them—the more of his face that was blocked from view, the better. So he hid outside and we went in and mingled.

"Hi, my name's Eddie, are you a doctor?"

"How do you do, I'm Ivy Sunday, I'll be playing drums for you tonight, is there anyone here in the medical profession?"

"Yeah, the name's Reese, hi, how ya doing, hope you like our music, say, I got something in my eye here, is there a doctor in the house?"

158

"'Evening, I'm Georgie Redding, thank you for having us. Listen, we're new in the neighborhood, can you recommend a good family doctor?"

Well, it wasn't subtle, but we had to move fast, and if the people were a little surprised at our questions, they forgot them fast when we started to play.

At one party (Shelby had on his hat, shades *and* J.D.'s scarf), the host jumped up in the middle of a set and cried, "Wait! Wait, before you play anything else—my kids are sleeping upstairs and I want them to come down and hear you!" And he ran up to get them.

That happened again. We were listened to by babies! Moms brought them out of their cribs, and they were terrific! They bounced up and down and gurgled at us and had a great time.

And we were making money.

"Here, Pop," I said one day.

"What's this, Eddie?"

"It's what I owe you for the keyboard."

Pop didn't say anything. He just raised his eyebrows and looked at me.

"That's a lot of money, Eddie," he said finally.

"Yeah, I know. Thanks for backing me."

"Eddie, you're a good boy." He kissed me on top of my head.

"Thanks, Pop."

"The garbage is in a bag near the back door. Take it out."

"Right, Pop." Even heroes have to take out the garbage.

❧

"I feel terrible," Shelby said one night as we were getting out of Mr. Sunday's truck.

"Why?"

"My parents said how nice it was I was getting asked to so many parties."

"Well, it *is*," Reese said.

"It makes me feel guilty."

"You ain't doin' nothin' wrong," Reese said.

"Well, you should know," Georgie said. He was always needling Reese who sometimes ignored him and sometimes didn't, depending on his mood. This time he ignored him.

"I mean it, Shel. There's nothin' wrong here. You're earning an honest buck playing music and havin' a good time. If your folks can't see that then it's their problem and not yours."

"That's what I keep telling myself, but I still feel guilty." He paused and we looked at him. "Not guilty enough to *stop*, though!" he finished and we laughed and headed for the house.

"I'll go around to the back door," Shelby said as usual.

"I'll let you in when it's clear," Ivy promised.

❧

By the end of February I felt nearly rich! We hadn't bombed out at one gig we played. All the people in their late twenties and thirties—they loved us, and they spread the word. Even Shelby began to relax a little. At all the parties and little concerts we played, not once did anyone seem to recognize him or even pick him out of the group, except to compliment him on his solos, the way they did with all of us. No one ever mentioned his father.

"See, Shel? You're safe. These folks move in different circles than your parents," Georgie said one night as we were waiting for one of the Sundays to pick us up.

"I guess so," Shelby said. "My parents don't go to parties where a live group plays blues. They go to cocktail parties where Bach is the background music."

"Yeah, and they're older, too," Ivy said. "These are kind of young-marrieds. With babies."

"Altogether a different socio-economic strata," Reese said.

Reese was sure weird. But he made Shelby take it a little easier.

Shel kept the hat, but he did forget about the shades and the scarf.

It was the beginning of March when Reese asked us his favor. And it took him forever to get to the point.

"Have to ask you something," he muttered at a Monday practice.

"What?" we said.

"A favor."

"Okay."

"It's a big favor."

"O-*kay.*"

"Probably you won't wanna do it."

"Probably not, Reese," Georgie said.

"What *is* it?" Ivy asked.

"Ah, forget it."

"Come *on,* Reese . . ." Ivy chopped her drumstick against her leg.

"Let's have it, Reese," Shelby said.

"Nah."

*"Reese!"* I yelled.

"It's my brother," he said.

We waited, but he didn't say anything.

"Reese, will you for Pete's sake *speak?*"

"It's his birthday next week."

"You want to get him a present?" I asked.

"Kind of."

"Well, sure! What?"

"I was thinking . . . Maybe we could play for him. At the jail. If they'll let us. Which they probably won't, but if they will, would you?"

We decoded that pretty quick.

"A concert at the jail! That's a great idea!" Ivy cried.

It took some work to convince other people it was a great idea. We called the jail and got turned down, but Reese thought of Father Ebert, who was the chaplain for the Department of Correction and Father Ebert talked to the warden and the recreation supervisor and convinced him and said that he, personally, would escort us and take us in, and generally be responsible for us. Since he'd done that before with church singing groups, they said it would be okay.

We set it up for the Friday night of Big Reese's birthday and it was going to be a surprise for him, we hoped. At least, we told Father Ebert to tell the warden not to say what the program in the gym was for.

Raymond Sunday drove us as usual and J.D. came along, too. All of us were very up, but Reese was like Desi Arnaz expecting his first baby on *I Love Lucy.* Instead of Georgie worrying about being late, it was Reese, although we were about a half-hour early getting together. Instead of Shelby worrying about being seen, it was Reese worrying about the instruments, the amps, the lights, the way we all looked.

"Knock it off, Reese," Georgie said finally. "We've done this before, y'know . . ."

"Not for him, we ain't," Reese answered.

"We'll be especially good for this one, Reese," Shelby told him. "I promise. We'll never be this good again."

"Oh, don't say that!" I wailed.

❧

When we arrived at the jail with Father Ebert, we peered through large glass doors which were opened with a buzzer that someone at the desk pressed. And then there were metal gates. We looked around wide-eyed as they slammed open and closed.

"Hi, there," an officer said. "You going to the gym, right? Kids for the concert?"

"Yes . . ."

"Okay. You'll have to put all your gear on this."

"All of it?"

"What is that?"

"Metal detector. Like at the airports? You know."

We had to empty our pockets and put our watches and stuff on benches. All our instruments and their cases were searched. It made us feel funny, I can tell you. All except Reese, I guess, who was used to it.

"Okay," the officer said after the search. "We'll take you into the gym and you can set up your equipment. Then we'll bring the men down in two shifts. Four cell blocks first, then five, okay, Father?"

Father Ebert said it was okay.

"Are we playing twice, Father?" I whispered.

"Yes, Eddie, there are too many men to bring in all at once."

"But this was really just for Big Reese . . ."

"I know, but it wouldn't be fair to exclude some of the inmates. Don't you want to do two shows?"

"Oh, yes! Sure, we do," I said.

We walked through a gate with a sign that said Cell Block West C-D above it, then two more gates and finally we saw the gym on our left.

"Wow!" Ivy said. "It's huge!"

"Yeah, it is," the officer said. "See, we pulled the bleachers over for you . . ."

We set everything up. Father Ebert found out that Big Reese's group would be coming down first and we were glad about that because we were fresh and ready to go.

We didn't recognize him, of course, but Reese did immediately and stood up on my stool with his buffalo-nickel guitar raised high above his head, almost like a special salute. Ivy looked over at me and bit her lip. I knew why, I felt shaky myself.

Father Ebert was the one elected to introduce us this time and while he was talking I looked down at my fingers, silently spread over the keyboard. Please, I said inside my head, please let this be the very best concert we ever played because it's so important to Reese and he hasn't had very much go right in his life, I guess, at least not the way the rest of us have had with nice families and all, so if we can make this really good I sure would be grateful, thanks a lot.

"—Nickel Blues *Band!*" Father Ebert finished and we went into our opening number, which was very special and a one-time only: *Happy Birthday to You* in a funky four-beat blues tempo.

165

Somehow, Reese got his brother to stand up so we could see him and then we played the rest of the concert directly to him. I guess we were just fine because I could see Big Reese take a slap at his cheek every now and then as if he were wiping away tears, but maybe that was just my imagination. His little brother was the one I was mostly concerned with and his face looked like Santa Claus had come down the chimney and handed him the world. I knew he was nervous but he never missed a beat, never lost his line, never got in the way. We gave a good concert! And when it was over we waved and the men waved and even Father Ebert waved.

We were exhausted before the second show. From emotion, mainly, I think, because usually we never felt too tired after we played.

"Thanks, you guys, thanks," Reese kept saying over and over.

"It was fun, Reese, we liked it," I kept trying to tell him, but he was too busy being grateful. I know how he felt because I know how it is when something means a lot to you and you want people to understand it but the words you say never seem like they're enough. And that's how Reese was acting.

Someone brought in orange juice for us while we were waiting for the next group and that revived us a little. By the time they came in we were ready to do a good show.

It was going over well (you can always tell an audience's reaction), when toward the end, an officer came in and went straight to Father Ebert and the warden. I could see them talking out of the corner of my eye. The warden frowned, nodded, and headed for the door, walking gingerly around our wires stretched out across the floor.

When we were finished, this group stood up and applauded, our first standing ovation! Boy, what that can make you feel like! They were still clapping when I edged up to Father Ebert.

"Where'd the warden go?" I asked. "Did something happen?"

"You've got sharp eyes, Eddie," Father Ebert said.

"Well, this place interests me," I said. "I've never been in jail before. I wanted to see if it's like it is on television."

"Nothing's like it is on television," Father Ebert said with a smile.

"Well, where *is* the warden?" I persisted.

"Nothing serious happened, Eddie. Nothing dramatic, at least not today. An appendicitis, we think. One of the men collapsed on his way back to his cell."

"Big Reese?"

"Reese? No. It was someone else."

"Oh!" I sighed with relief. I didn't want anything to spoil Reese's day.

We waited until the gym was clear and then J.D.

and Raymond began to help us collect our stuff.

We felt fine as the officers and Father Ebert and everyone told us how much they'd enjoyed the concert and we said we hoped they'd let us back there to perform again. We told the warden that everything we did was arranged by Big Reese and the warden laughed.

"Everyone here knows that, Eddie!" he boomed.

A gate opened suddenly and we moved against the wall as a stretcher was carried toward the door.

"Ah," the warden said, addressing a tall black man in a suit. "Appendix after all, eh, Doc?"

"Appendix, after all," the doctor said. He smiled at us kids. Then he gaped at us. *"Shelby?"* he cried.

*"Dad!"*

# 13.

That's how it all ended.

All those precautions we took for every party we played and here where we figured we were safe . . . The next day, I called him.

"What's going on, Shel?"

"I can't talk long, Eddie, I'm grounded for life!" he whispered into the phone.

"What was your father doing there, for Pete's sake?"

"It was an emergency. They called him. He used to work there once a week when we first moved here, but he hasn't in years. I don't know, I guess they couldn't reach the regular—"

"But what happens now, Shel?"

"Aw, Eddie, I'm sorry. I don't think I'll ever get out of my room again."

"Shelby—"

"No, look, Eddie. Where this is concerned, my mother has a blind spot the size of New Jersey. I hate to fight her on it because all she remembers is the lousy life she thinks she had. But, Eddie—I didn't mention this—"

"What?"

"There's a state-wide brass festival coming up in the spring. Larzo's preparing me for it and even though I'm underage, there's a chance I could get to perform with a symphony orchestra if I do well. Eddie?"

"I'm here."

"So you see, I have to spend a lot of time getting ready for it. I really should have been practicing for this after school instead of—"

"Instead of the blues."

"Yeah. Instead of the blues. I'm sorry, Eddie."

Unhappily, J.D. cancelled the other jobs he'd gotten for us. The music wouldn't be the same without the horn, without Shelby. We'd have to re-learn everything, and in a different style, and we just didn't have the heart for it.

Especially poor Ivy.

Sweet, sunny, happy Ivy turned into "Gloomy Sunday," the title of that old Billie Holiday tune. That's what I called her, Gloomy Sunday.

"Knock it off, Eddie," she said wearily.

"But look at you, Ivy, your whole personality's changing!"

"Well, but the band broke up and I don't ever see Shelby outside of school any more . . ."

I understood. I felt awful about losing the band, but Ivy had double trouble, losing Shelby, too.

Toward the end of March, Georgie came up to me in the hall at school.

"Listen, Eddie, Zach Beecher asked me if I'd be interested in playing with his group."

"Rock, Georgie?"

Georgie looked sheepish. His freckles all stood out extra brown. "Yeah," he said. "I just want to keep playing, you know, even if it's not my favorite kind of music any more."

"Well, yeah, Georgie, you should."

"We can still get together and practice sometimes," he said.

"Sure," I said. I knew what he meant. I don't think I'd've played rock anywhere because I don't like it, but I wanted to keep playing, too. Only I wasn't sure at what, or where . . .

"Hey, Eddie!"

"Reese! What are you doing *inside* school?"

"Finally got caught. Last week."

"How do you like it?" I asked.

"It's different," he sniffed. "But guess what? I got a job!"

"Playing?"

"No, not yet. At Ettinger's. After school. I work behind the counter. And Mr. Ettinger says since I know guitars I can help sell."

"An honest job, Reese? You got rehabilitated?"

He ignored that. "In return for the work, I get lessons. Part of my money Mr. Ettinger uses for lessons." Ettinger's gives music lessons in little studios in back of the store. "And I can still pay Shelby back a little at a time."

"That's terrific, Reese!" I said.

He said, "Yeah. The straight life. Would you believe it?"

"I'd believe it. I've been leading it for years."

"Yeah. I'll let you know if I get tired of it. See ya, Eddie."

"See ya, Reese."

❧

Shelby would be okay, I figured. Reese and Georgie were finding different roads. It was my turn next.

Of course I kept up with my piano lessons, but I did switch back to Tuesdays to make it easier on my mother with Yvonne's lessons still on Tuesday and all. As Ham pointed out, learning is never wasted even if you don't use every bit of it every minute. I guess I'll still be studying piano when I'm bald like my father and have kids of my own.

My turn to take a different road came when I handed in an English assignment and Mr. Latella said, "Say, Eddie, you in on this seventh-grade revolt?"

"What revolt?"

"The June show instead of the annual Chorale?"

"No, Mr. Latella . . ."

"Oh. I just heard about it a day or so ago. Seems your student council voted down the annual Chorale in favor of an original seventh-grade revue."

"I hadn't heard about it," I said. But I would.

The committee who "revolted" consisted of a bunch of kids in the Chorale who were tired of singing *An Artist's Life* and *On the Road to Mandalay*. They wanted to do an original musical—a parody on what it's like to enter junior high for the first time. With a take-off on the teachers, too. I scouted them down and asked if they could use a musical director. And then I had a new job, too!

We only had two-and-a-half months and I never worked so hard in my life. Not only did I have the show, I had my bar mitzvah coming up, so I had two things to get nervous about, plus I had my special speech to write, the one at the end of the ceremony where the bar mitzvah boy pledges his continuing religious study and thanks his parents and family and all that, *and* I was also writing the school show.

The way that worked out was, we wrote the thing as we went along, taking everybody's ideas as they came up. I mean, we started with an outline, of course, but then as the kids got into it, they each had something to offer and if it worked, then we kept it in. One time, part of my bar mitzvah speech accidentally got into the show script and everyone wanted to leave it in. I didn't let them, though, because then my parents would have heard it before the ceremony, and besides, it really wasn't supposed to be funny.

For the music of the show, we used popular and Broadway songs and we put our own words to them. The show was all about how insignificant seventh graders feel after they were the big cheeses in elementary school. There they are in a big junior high and they're considered nothing, zip, wormlike, zero by the other kids and by the teachers. Just another number on computerized report cards.

Our opening number was called *A Seventh Grader Is the Lowest Form of Life;* the boys did a kick-line chorus to it. And the finale was this dream sequence, where the seventh-grader, played by Marvin Willingham who looks just like his name, imagines he finally gets out of Worthlessville by graduating from college and then finds he's just landed back there again when he learns he's just a trainee at his new job.

Well, the Broadway composers won't have to worry about us, but it wasn't too bad. As I said, I never had so much work.

Luckily, the show came before my bar mitzvah and I was really glad about that because I wanted to be able to relax at least for a few days and go over my speech and the prayers and everything else in relative peace and quiet.

Ivy was asked, but she didn't play drums in the show. She went out for girls' soccer, and even though she tried out late, she made the team. I guess Ivy'd probably be good at anything she wanted badly enough.

"Congratulations," I said when she told me.

"Thanks, Eddie . . ."

"Aren't you playing at all, Ivy?"

"I don't want to for a while, Eddie. I think I need a real change. And I like playing soccer . . . We get to go to different schools and everything. I won't give the drums up . . . only for a while."

Yeah. For a while. I still got a twinge sometimes at night when I thought about the band, the wonderful Buffalo Nickel Blues Band. Each of us was into something new now, but it wasn't gradual like I'd always figured it would be. We had been so close and come such a long way together in what was really such a short time . . .

No one was surprised when Shelby scored high at his brass festival. His teacher told him he was sure he'd be invited to play with a symphony, even though he was so young. Symphony orchestras do that with real talented kids, although they're usually in high school by the time they hit that mark.

And of course, Shel came to the show. All the band did and when I took my bow, last, when the kids pulled me up on the stage, Ivy ran down the aisle and threw a yellow rose at me!

It was a good night, a fun night as all the performing nights and days were. But gee . . . I guess there's nothing like the feeling of playing with your first band . . .

The Friday night before your bar mitzvah, it's required for the celebrant to help conduct the service at the temple. It isn't hard, I'd been to lots of services, naturally, and anyway you have to go to services at least twice a month the year of your bar mitzvah. So I was kind of surprised when my parents made such a big deal out of my performance.

"Wait'll tomorrow," I said. "That's really the big deal."

The bar mitzvah was at the temple, but the reception was at my house. Outdoors. No one could believe my mother planned a reception for about eighty people outdoors.

"What if it rains?" Aunt Rosalie wanted to know, the week before.

"It won't," my mother said.

"I can't believe you're doing this. Aren't you at least going to have a tent?"

"It won't rain. A tent would take up the whole backyard."

"You can't have a rain date, you know. A bar mitzvah is a bar mitzvah. Are you prepared to have eighty people in your living room? Ha!"

"It won't rain," my mother said.

Of course it didn't. It was gorgeous. Not too hot, sunny. Perfect. Just like my mother ordered.

"You're going to be wonderful," she said to me as we were leaving for the temple. "I'm so proud of you. And if you can find Dr. Broigen in the congregation, smile at him."

176

"Mr. Broigen?"

"*Doctor.* Don't be mean, Eddie, he's giving up his tree blight for a day to come to your bar mitzvah."

"You invited him? Why?"

"Because he's sacrificing all his time so we can have chestnut trees. Because he's our *neighbor,* that's why, why do you think? And anyway, he thought you were very ingenious to have sound-proofed your practicing place for him the way you did."

"But *I* didn't—"

"Sh!"

On the way to the temple, my sister Yvonne asked me if I was nervous. I said, "Of course not!" but I was.

I also felt badly that on my big day only two Buffalo Nickels would be there to share it with me: Ivy and Georgie. Well, that was nice, because we were together first—the Centerin City Blues Trio—but still, I knew I'd miss Shelby and Reese. Shelby had an audition in New York and Reese said he had something or other to do with his sister. I wondered if it was because he couldn't get himself another suit to wear. I would have told him to wear any darn thing he pleased, except he didn't use that as an excuse so I couldn't very well excuse it.

Anyway, I knew J.D. Ettinger would be there. And of course, Ham, who would put on his first suit, he said, in years! And maybe even ol' Dr.—Mr. Broigen! They'd all be there to cut themselves globs of the chopped-liver piano that Aunt Rosalie finally learned how to make!

First came the regular service and prayers which took just enough time to take my stomach from a low growl to a full-fledged chorus. I was never that nervous when I was playing piano!

I was also the only one getting bar mitzvah'd that day, too. The other kids in my Hebrew class had either done it or were doing it later on in the year.

My chanting turned out okay. By the time we got to that part I'd been up there enough time to feel better and my stomach didn't sing along with me like I'd been afraid it would. The cantor smiled at me and so by the time I read the haf torah, which is what you read on your Hebrew birthday, I was actually pretty calm. The only hitch was that my voice cracked embarrassingly during my big thanking-everybody speech but when the cantor still smiled I guessed he was glad it hadn't happened during my prayer chants.

As I looked out at the congregation, I could see my mother in the front row mopping her eyes with my father's big white handkerchief, not the little tan lace one it took her a month to pick out. It made me think of seeing her in the audience a year before at our party. She made me feel proud.

My sister Yvonne waved at me by wiggling her fingers and I smiled back at her and nodded.

It was strange, standing up there before an audience instead of sitting down at a keyboard and I thought—even though my birthday wouldn't be for another two weeks, the bar mitzvah ceremony made me officially—a man.

We went back to our house as soon as it was over. I felt like a real king, with all the congratulations and pats on the back I was getting.

Even Dr.—Mr. Broigen was there. He patted me lightly on the head and said, "Well done. Well done." I wondered if he'd noticed that there were no more musicians going into the garage—or music coming out of it.

I went into the kitchen to thank my mother again and did a double-take out the kitchen window.

"Ma! What's that in the yard?"

"Don't say 'what's that', she'll hear you. That's the rabbi's wife's hat."

"Not that, not the hat. Those! Over there, in the corner of the yard!"

My mother came over to the window. "Where?" she said, peering.

"Ma! The instruments! All set up over there!"

"Oh. That. That's for the entertainment."

"*What* entertainment? You never said anything about entertainment! Besides . . . that's my keyboard! And Ivy's drums, too!"

"So?"

"Ma . . ."

"Come outside, Eddie."

My mother took me by the hand, which normally I would not have let her do, especially since I was officially a man, but I was so bewildered and confused I just followed along like a kid.

"Everybody!" my mother called. "Everybody!"

When she said that, the guests milling around the backyard all got quiet and when I looked over at the corner where the instruments were, I saw that each of their players were in place: Ivy, grinning at me from her seat behind her drums; Georgie, nodding, holding his guitar; Reese, waving at me with the neck of his guitar; Shelby, who did a low bow, sweeping his horn in front of him. And it was J.D. Ettinger who started the applause.

Imagine how it feels when you're supposed to be a man and you practically bust out crying in front of all your relatives!

"Attention, everybody!" my mother called. "I'm happy to present to you—the popular, terrific and marvelous—Buffalo Nickel Blues Band!"

I walked to the keyboard, dazed.

"We haven't practiced," I mouthed at the group, but they just waved hands at me as if to say, it's okay, we'll do okay.

We sat down and I called out a tune—I can't even remember now what it was—but when Ivy set the tempo, the sound of her brushes seemed to send electricity all through me and it must have been contagious because the group never sounded better. Great new ideas just kept pouring out from each and every one of us, it was so beautiful! There was Uncle Mike, smiling and tapping his foot . . . Even Alice and Andrew stayed perfectly still and listened. I had a wonderful time.

❦

"How'd you get here, Shel?" I asked when we finally stopped playing and had a chance to eat.

"Well . . ." he said, "I lied about my audition. It's not for another two days. We all wanted to surprise you."

"But how about playing with us?"

"Oh, that was your mother," he mumbled through a mouthful of chopped liver. "She talked to my mother for two hours. I never knew anyone could drink one cup of coffee for that long. That's all she said she was coming over for, one cup of coffee."

"Yeah, that's Ma."

"My mother's still dead set against my playing pop. But this was such a special occasion she just couldn't refuse."

"I'm glad, Shel. And maybe if one time was okay, there might be other times. Later on."

"Yeah, maybe. But I sure wouldn't have missed this, Eddie."

"Thanks," I said and we shook hands.

Big Reese got out of the slammer in August. Just like his brother, he got a job at Ettinger's which worked out great, since the brothers could look after each other and J.D. could look after them both! When Reese went back to school in the fall, Big Reese and the Ettingers made sure he stayed there.

Shelby's in the city a lot of the time. He works very hard on his music and has played with the Florida Symphony. You'll hear his name someday, he's going to be famous, I'm sure. (That is, if you like classical music.)

Georgie still plays with Zach Beecher's rock band and he also went out for track in the fall. He got very tall all of a sudden.

Ivy. Ivy got so grown up. Here I was the one supposed to be a man, but I felt exactly the same as I always did. Ivy was the one who was different. She didn't play soccer in the fall, but she did try out for cheerleading and made it. Naturally. And there's a boy on the football team I see her with after the games. The days of our being best friends are gone but I believe that we'll never forget each other. Never.

Me. Well, I'm still taking lessons from Ham and I'm learning to conduct a chorus after school. The music teacher's helping me and I think I like it even better than playing, sometimes. When you pick up your arms and the voices begin to sing—I can't explain it, but you feel like you yourself are an instrument. It's very interesting.

J.D. Ettinger's still hustling and wheeling and dealing. My mother told him his next manager's assignment is to get my sister Yvonne into the American Ballet Company. I told her J.D. would be able to part the Red Sea first!

The Buffalo Nickels. I'll never forget them. We were amazing. But I know I'm different in one way: Instead of thinking that when something's going good, it's going to go on forever—now I think: I wonder what's going to happen to me tomorrow? I guess that's what happens when you're not a kid any more. You just have to be ready for anything.

3908　15

F　　Angell, Judie
ANG
　　　The Buffalo Nickel
　　　Blues Band

| DATE | | | |
|------|--|--|--|
| APR 16 '94 | | | |
| | | | |
| SEP 2 | | | |
| SEP 23 '91 | | | |
| SEP 30 '92 | | | |
| NOV 12 '82 | | | |
| JAN 24 95 | | | |
| | | | |
| | | | |
| | | | |